BLOOD RITUAL

TRINITY OF THORNS

ALEXANDER MORGAN

COVER DESIGN
RHIANNON LOUISE ADEY

Published UK 2024
First Edition

All rights reserved, including the right to reproduce this book or portions thereof in any form whatsoever. For information, address the publisher.

ISBN 978-1-0683320-0-5

To My Dad,

It's only now, as an adult, that I truly understand the sacrifices you made to provide me with everything I had growing up. Thank you for everything.

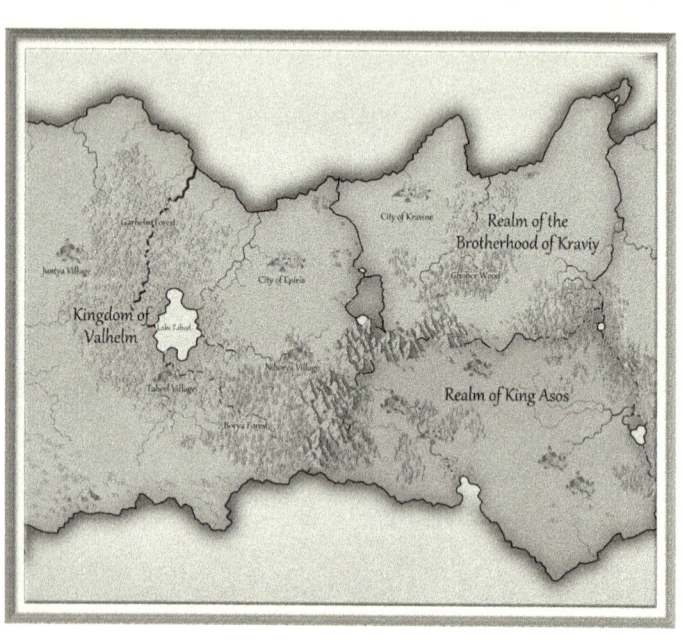

Prologue

Winter 1307 Niborya Village

The village of Niborya burned, its once-familiar streets now a tangle of smoke, ash, and death. Casius clutched Arla's hand tightly, his palm slick with sweat and dirt as he pulled her through the chaos. The air reeked of charred wood and spilled blood, every step threatened to reveal them to the soldiers who prowled the alleys like wolves.

"Casius, my ankle…" Arla whimpered, stumbling as she tried to keep up. Her small frame shuddered with each laboured step, her face streaked with soot and tears.

"Quiet!" Casius hissed, his voice sharper than he intended. He glanced over his shoulder, guilt twisting in his chest at the sight of her tear-streaked face. "Just a little further, okay? We'll be safe soon."

The lie tasted bitter.

Around them, the village was unrecognisable. Homes were reduced to smouldering skeletons of timber, their walls caving inward as flames devoured them. Bodies lay strewn across the cobblestones, some twisted in unnatural shapes, others crumpled as though they'd simply stopped running.

Casius kept them low, darting between the rubble and the shadows. The heavy clink of armour and the bark of orders drifted closer, soldiers moving methodically through the streets. Somewhere behind them, a woman's scream tore through the night, cut off abruptly.

"Casius," Arla whispered, pulling at his sleeve. "Where's Mama?"

Casius didn't answer. He couldn't. His throat tightened as he thought of their mother's face, pale and urgent as she'd shoved them toward the back door of their house. *Run,* she'd said. *Don't look back.*

He'd wanted to fight. He'd wanted to stay. But the fear in her eyes had burned into him more deeply than the flames now eating their home. He'd taken Arla's hand, his father's bow and run.

Now, the reality of her absence weighed on him like a stone.

"Casius!" Arla tugged again, her voice breaking with desperation. "Where's Mama?"

"She's coming," he lied, his voice tight. "She'll find us. But we have to keep moving. Come on."

They slipped through a narrow alley, ducking beneath a sagging wooden beam as ash drifted around them like snow. On the far side, the village square came into view. Casius froze, pulling Arla back into the shadows.

The square, once the heart of Niborya, was a scene of horror. Flames licked at the edges of the thatched roofs surrounding it, casting flickering light on the dozen or so soldiers gathered in a loose semicircle. Their armour was grimy, swords already slick with blood.

And in the centre, on her knees in the dirt, was Anais.

Casius felt his breath catch, his chest tightening painfully. He pushed Arla behind him, shielding her from the sight, though her small hands clutched at his shirt as she peeked around him.

"Mama," she whispered, her voice trembling.

Anais's hands were bound behind her back, her dark hair falling in tangled waves over her shoulders. Soot streaked her face, but her eyes burned with defiance as she turned glaring up at the man pacing behind her.

Casius's gaze locked onto the man immediately. He wasn't dressed like the other soldiers. Instead of armour, he wore a long, weathered coat that swept around his boots as he moved. A finely crafted blade hung at his side, its polished edge gleaming in the firelight. His face was sharp and gaunt, a deep scar cutting through his left brow and disappearing into the stubble on his cheek.

The man's voice was calm, almost conversational, but it carried through the square with ease. "Where are they?"

Anais didn't answer.

He crouched beside her, his gloved hand tilting her chin upward so their eyes met. "You've already lost everything you care for. Tell me where they are, and I'll make it quick."

Anais spat at him, her voice trembling but fierce. "You'll never find them."

The man sighed, standing and drawing his blade in one fluid motion. "Wrong answer."

"No" Casius whispered, his voice breaking. He started to move forward, but Arla clung to him desperately.

"Don't!" she cried, her voice high and panicked.

Her small hands held him back, and the weight of her presence. Their mother's final command rooted him to the spot. Tears streamed down his face as he watched the man grip Anais by the hair, tilting her head back.

"Don't look," Casius whispered, pulling Arla's face into his chest.

The blade flashed, and Anais slumped forward, her lifeless body crumpling to the ground. Blood pooled beneath her, gushing from the opening in her throat, the firelight reflecting in the growing stain.

Casius's breath came in shallow gasps, his vision blurring as his tears mingled with the smoke. His mother's final moments seared into his memory like a brand.

"Burn the rest," the man said coldly, sheathing his blade. "And find the brats. They can't have gone far."

"Yes, Captain," one of the soldiers replied.

Casius didn't wait to hear more. Grabbing Arla, he turned and bolted for the trees, his legs trembling beneath him as he stumbled over roots and rubble.

They reached the treeline as the first stars began to peek through the smoke-filled sky. The sounds of the village faded behind them, replaced by the rustling of leaves and the distant calls of night birds.

Casius stopped, his chest heaving as he set Arla down. She was crying quietly, her face streaked with soot and tears.

"Mama…" she whimpered, clutching at his tunic.

Casius knelt in front of her, gripping her shoulders gently but firmly. "Arla," he said, his voice shaking. "Mama's… she's not coming. Do you understand?"

She shook her head, fresh tears spilling over her cheeks. "No! She'll find us. She promised—"

"She's gone!" Casius snapped, his voice breaking. Arla flinched, her wide eyes staring up at him. Guilt immediately flared in his chest, and he pulled her into a hug.

"I'm sorry," he murmured, his voice softening. "I'm so sorry. But it's just us now, Arla. We have to be strong. For her."

Arla sniffled, her small hands clutching at him. "I want Mama," she whispered.

"So do I," he said, his tears spilling freely. "But she... she wanted us to get away. That's what we have to do. We have to keep going."

Arla nodded reluctantly, wiping her nose on the sleeve of her dress.

Chapter 1

Spring 1308 Eastern Bank of Lake Taheel, Prince's Marching Camp

A day's ride from the city of Epiris, the heir to the throne and his royal bodyguard arrived at the marching camp stationed by the southern shore of Lake Taheel. Fresh orders from the King had cast an air of anticipation over the soldiers. Whispers of danger spread like wildfire, reports of enemy movement in the forests, roadside traders found dead and stripped of anything valuable. Unease rippled through the ranks, a silent current beneath the surface.

At the heart of the camp lay a central clearing, where two hundred men of Prince Althern's army stood to attention, their posture stiff and resolute. The forest surrounding the camp was alive with the morning's natural chorus, birdsong weaving through the crisp air, broken occasionally by the barked orders of officers. The camp, though apprehensive about potential action, buzzed with the disciplined energy of soldiers ready to serve.

When Prince Althern and his thirty mounted bodyguards rode into the square, the men's backs straightened even further. Althern was no stranger to the battlefield. Though only thirty summers old, he had proven himself a warrior of unmatched skill, having defended the King's throne in decisive victories against enemies both foreign and domestic.

At the head of his formation, Althern reigned in his steed. The sunlight gleamed off his polished armour, giving him an almost otherworldly presence. His horse snorted, its breath misting in the cool air.

"Early start for the men, Grand Marshal Pesus," Althern remarked, his tone measured.

The Prince dismounted gracefully, handing his reins to a nearby soldier. Walking at an unhurried pace, he began weaving through the assembled lines, his sharp eyes studying each man in turn.

Toward the end of the second row, Althern stopped abruptly. His gaze fixed on a young soldier who stood out—not for any remarkable quality, but for what was missing.

"Soldier," Althern said, his voice sharp enough to draw the attention of everyone nearby, "you appear to have replaced your sword with a hunting knife for this morning's parade."

The young man flinched as the Prince reached forward, drawing the knife from its sheath. He remained rigid, his eyes fixed somewhere beyond Althern's shoulder, clearly afraid to meet his gaze.

The blade was simple—a hunting knife with a horn handle. But it was in impeccable condition, honed to a deadly point. Althern turned it over in his hand, inspecting it with quiet intensity before speaking again.

"Your name, soldier?"

The young man shifted slightly, his weight moving from one foot to the other. "Pax, Sire," he replied, his voice firm but quiet.

"And where is your sword, Pax?"

Pax hesitated, his face reddening. "I don't have one, my

Lord. I… I can't afford one. My family has no money." His voice trailed off, embarrassment plain in his expression.

Althern's eyes narrowed as he considered the boy's response. After a moment, he spoke again, his tone sharp but not unkind.

"Pax, how will you defend your brothers with no sword? How will you fight for my honour—or the honour of your King—without the most basic equipment? Do you hope to one day make a knight?"

The young soldier swallowed hard, his breathing shallow. He stood in the front ranks, one of the newest and poorest men under Althern's command. These front ranks were often filled with men like Pax—those who came from nothing, providing their own meagre equipment and risking their lives for the slim chance of becoming a knight. The mortality rate was high, but the promise of glory and immortality as one of the King's chosen knights kept the supply of hopefuls steady.

"I… I will defend my brothers and my King with my bare hands if I have to," Pax said finally, his voice trembling with suppressed emotion. He opened his mouth to say more but faltered, instead clenching his jaw and fixing his gaze once more on the trees behind Althern.

Althern studied him for another moment, then returned the knife to its sheath. "Meet me at the command tent after the parade," he said curtly. "A man without the tools of war is no good to me—or this army."

Pax deflated visibly, his shoulders sagging. His fellow soldiers cast sidelong glances at him, some sympathetic, others indifferent.

Little did Althern know the lengths Pax had gone to just to stand in this formation.

Pax's father had been a blacksmith, but foreign traders bringing cheaper arms into Epiris had driven him out of work.

With no income, the family had struggled to make ends meet. Pax, desperate not to become a burden, had left Juntya, his small village, under the cover of twilight. He had no horse, no armour, and only the hunting knife at his side. For three days, he had walked the long road to Epiris, driven by sheer determination and the hope of a better future.

Now, standing in front of his Prince, Pax felt the sting of failure.

Grand Marshal Pesus, a hulking figure clad in full armour, approached Althern, his face set in a grim frown. His rough, gravelly voice carried easily over the murmurs of the soldiers.

"I apologise, Sire," Pesus said, throwing a irritated glance at Pax. "That one slipped the net. I'll address it immediately. You won't have to see him again."

Althern raised a hand dismissively, his expression thoughtful. "No need, Grand Marshal. The command tent. All officers. We have new orders."

Pesus hesitated, his eyes narrowing slightly as he watched Althern stride away. Then, with a nod, he turned back to the formation. "Get back in line," he barked at Pax before following the Prince.

As the Prince disappeared toward the command tent, the army stood in silence, awaiting further orders.

Pax remained in the front ranks, where one hundred and twenty young men like him stood, their armour mismatched and their weapons often second-hand. Behind them were sixty knights, their gleaming uniforms a stark contrast to the front ranks' humble gear. Each knight wore the King's colours proudly, their weapons and armour marking them as professionals.

At the rear were the archers—twenty highly skilled

bowmen who doubled as hunters and scouts, their precision essential for keeping the army fed and their enemies at bay.

Finally, there was Althern's bodyguard: thirty mounted heavy cavalry, their polished armour and powerful warhorses forming a shining wall of authority. They represented the strength and prestige of Epiris, a reminder of what the front ranks aspired to become. The army was a patrol army, a portion of Epiris men who went with either the Grand Marshal or Prince Althern checking on the borders and towns of the Kingdom.

As the parade concluded, the men began to disperse, whispers rippling through the ranks about what new orders the Prince might have brought.

Pax stood in silence, his mind racing. He glanced once more at the trees behind him, his determination hardening.

Chapter 2

Spring 1308 West of Niborya

The forest loomed dense and shadowed, its canopy thick enough to block out much of the fading evening light. Every branch seemed to claw at them, every sound an echo of their flight from Niborya. Casius led the way, his hand clutching Arla's smaller one tightly. Her breathing was shallow, each step punctuated by a wince that made his stomach churn.

"Not much further," Casius said, though he had no idea how far they had to go. His voice wavered despite himself. He tightened his grip on Arla's hand, trying to sound convincing. "Once we get to Lake Taheel, we'll be safe."

Arla limped behind him, her injured ankle slowing them down. The bandage he had hastily tied around it back in the village had loosened, dirt smearing the cloth. Her face was pale, streaked with grime and dried tears. She stumbled over a root, and Casius quickly caught her before she hit the ground.

"I'm fine," she muttered, though her voice was no stronger than a whisper.

"No, you're not." He crouched in front of her, his hands

gripping her shoulders. "We'll stop here for a bit. Let me check your ankle."

Arla shook her head, her lips trembling. "We can't stop. What if... what if they're still following us?"

Casius hesitated, scanning the darkened forest around them. His ears strained for any sound of pursuit—the snapping of twigs, the clink of armour—but the only noises were the rustling of leaves and the distant hoot of an owl. Even so, the thought of the enemy soldiers still hunting them sent a cold shiver down his spine.

"We're far enough now," he lied gently. "They won't find us tonight."

Reluctantly, Arla sat on a fallen log, wincing as she stretched her injured leg. Casius knelt, untying the frayed strip of cloth and inspecting her swollen ankle. The skin was red and puffy, the bruise spreading up her shin.

"Does it hurt a lot?" he asked, his voice quieter now.

Arla shrugged. "Not as much as when it happened." But her eyes betrayed her, glistening with unshed tears.

Casius sighed and reached for the small satchel he'd grabbed during their escape. It contained some berries he'd foraged earlier, a handful of nuts, and an old waterskin that was nearly empty. He pulled out a few of the berries and handed them to her.

"Here, eat these. They'll help," he said, though even he wasn't sure if they were safe. The berries had a slightly bitter smell, and their pale red skin didn't match the ones his mother had once pointed out as edible.

Arla eyed them suspiciously. "Are you sure these aren't poison?"

Casius forced a grin, trying to mask his uncertainty. "Of course I'm sure. I wouldn't give you anything bad."

She hesitated but eventually popped one into her mouth,

chewing slowly. After a moment, her face scrunched up in disgust. "These taste awful."

Casius let out a weak laugh, relief flooding him that they didn't seem to be toxic. "Then they must be good for you."

Arla didn't laugh, her tired eyes drooping as she leaned against the log. Her exhaustion was palpable, and Casius's chest tightened as he watched her fight to stay awake.

He stood and scanned the forest again, his hands clenching into fists. Every shadow felt like a threat, every rustle of leaves a phantom of their pursuers. He couldn't let his guard down—not when Arla was depending on him. But the weight of it all pressed heavily on his shoulders. He was only fifteen. He didn't know how to keep them safe, not really. His mother had always been the one who knew what to do, and now she was gone.

The memory of her death hit him like a blade to the gut. He saw her face again, pale but defiant as Widow had stood over her. The sound of her scream, the sickening gurgle as the blade slashed her throat—it played over and over in his mind, a torment he couldn't escape.

"I should've done something," he whispered to himself, his voice trembling.

Arla stirred, her eyes half-opening. "What?"

Casius froze, realising he'd spoken aloud. He forced a weak smile, shaking his head. "Nothing. Just... thinking."

She sat up slightly, her voice small. "Do you think Mum's... still back there? In the village?"

Casius's throat tightened. He knelt beside her, his hands gripping hers. "Arla... Mum isn't coming back. She can't."

Arla's eyes widened, and for a moment, she looked like she might cry. But then she shook her head furiously. "No. She'll come. She always does. She always finds us."

Casius's heart broke at the hope in her voice. He wanted

to tell her she was right, that their mother would walk out of the woods any moment and scoop them into her arms. But he couldn't lie. Not about this.

"She wanted us to get away," he said softly, his voice thick with emotion. "She... she stayed so we could escape. She saved us, Arla. That's what she wanted."

Arla stared at him, her lip trembling. "But... I didn't say goodbye."

Casius pulled her into a hug, holding her tightly as her small frame shook with quiet sobs. "I didn't either," he murmured. "But we're going to make it, okay? For her. We'll get to the lake, and we'll be safe. That's what she wanted."

They stayed like that for a while, the forest growing darker around them. When Arla's sobs subsided, she sniffled and pulled back, wiping her nose on her sleeve.

"I'm thirsty," she said quietly.

Casius nodded, grabbing the waterskin from the satchel. He handed it to her, watching as she drank the last few drops. His stomach clenched. They needed more water. And food. The berries wouldn't last long, and he doubted he'd picked the right ones.

"We'll find something," he said, more to himself than to Arla. "Come on. We need to keep moving."

They walked slowly through the forest, Casius supporting Arla as she limped along. The night was cool, the air thick with the earthy smell of moss and damp leaves. They came across a small stream, its water dark and brackish. Casius hesitated, knowing it wasn't safe to drink. But Arla's parched throat pushed his doubts aside.

"Just a little," he said, cupping the water in his hands and offering it to her. "Not too much."

Arla drank reluctantly, wrinkling her nose at the taste. Casius took a sip himself, grimacing as the gritty liquid slid down his throat. It wasn't much, but it was better than nothing.

Casius knelt at the edge of the stream, cupping the cold water in his hands and splashing it onto his face. Arla wandered a little farther downstream, splashing through the burbling water. The forest seemed still for a moment—too still. A low, rumbling growl broke the silence, and Casius froze. Slowly, he turned his head, his heart thundering in his chest. Across the stream, half-hidden in the underbrush, a pair of yellow eyes glowed, locked on them with predatory intent. A wolf—thin, with matted fur and ribs visible beneath its hide—stepped forward, its lips curled back to reveal sharp, yellowed teeth.

"Arla," Casius whispered, keeping his voice steady as he rose to his feet. "Step back. Slowly."

Arla looked up, her eyes widening in terror as the wolf let out another growl, its muscles tensing. Casius put himself in front of Arla as a shield, nocking an arrow in his fathers bow, he locked eyes with the predator. His breathing heavy, he pulled back on the bow, his arm shaking slightly under the strain.

Another low, guttural growl came from behind them. Casius froze, his body stiff with fear as he turned slowly toward the sound. His breath caught as he saw a flash of movement in the shadows, and the underbrush shifted. His heart pounded, a wild drumbeat in his chest.

Suddenly, a brilliant white light burst into the clearing, forcing him to raise an arm to shield his eyes. The radiance wasn't blinding for long, though—it softened into a glow, revealing the unmistakable form of the white wolf. Its pristine coat shimmered in the dim light of the forest, its golden eyes calm and purposeful as it padded forward.

Casius flinched, taking a step back as the wolf passed just

inches from him. But it didn't seem to notice him or Arla. Its gaze was fixed on the wild predator crouched across the stream, teeth bared. The white wolf moved with deliberate grace, its steps soundless despite the damp leaves underfoot.

The wild wolf hesitated, its yellow eyes flicking between the white wolf and the children. It growled once more, a feeble attempt at dominance, but as the white wolf stopped and fixed it with an unblinking stare, the predator faltered. With a whimper, it turned tail, crashing through the underbrush in a frantic retreat.

The clearing fell silent, save for the rustle of leaves in the breeze and the trickling of the stream. The white wolf turned to face them, its golden eyes soft but commanding.

"You cannot stay here," it said, its voice clear and resonant, like the hum of the earth itself. "The forest is not safe for you. Move west, there humans own the land, not the wildlife."

Arla, wide-eyed, took a hesitant step toward the wolf, but Casius placed a hand on her shoulder. "Thank you," he said softly, his voice trembling with awe.

The wolf's eyes met his gaze, then turned and padded back into the forest. Its luminous form faded into the shadows, the glow gradually dimming until it disappeared completely.

Casius exhaled, realising he'd been holding his breath. He glanced down at Arla, who clung to his side, her small fingers gripping his tunic tightly. "Come on," he murmured, helping her to her feet. "We have to keep moving."

Arla nodded, her trust in him unwavering. Together, they left the stream behind, pressing deeper into the woods, the memory of the white wolf's presence a small spark of courage against the vast unknown.

They pressed on until the forest began to thin, the ground

sloping downward. The faint glimmer of water appeared through the trees, and Casius's chest tightened with relief.

"Lake Taheel," he said, pointing ahead. "We made it."

The lake stretched wide and calm under the moonlight, its surface reflecting the stars above. A small fishing hut stood at the water's edge, its windows dark. Nearby, nets were stretched across wooden poles, heavy with fish. Casius's stomach growled at the sight.

"Stay here," he whispered to Arla, helping her sit on a rock. "I'll get us something."

He crept toward the nets, his heart pounding. Every step felt too loud, every shadow a potential threat. When he reached the nets, he worked quickly, prying free a few fish and wrapping them in his tunic. He glanced at the hut, half-expecting someone to burst out and catch him, but the door remained shut.

Returning to Arla, he showed her the fish with a triumphant grin. "Dinner."

She managed a small smile, though her exhaustion was clear. Together, they disappeared into the woods once more, finding a small hollow where they could rest. Casius didn't dare light a fire, so they ate the fish raw, their hunger outweighing their discomfort.

As Arla curled up beside him, her head resting against his side, Casius stared out at the dark forest. His mother's voice echoed faintly in his mind, urging him to keep going. For Arla. For their future.

"Don't worry," he whispered, brushing a strand of hair from her face. "I'll keep you safe. I promise."

Chapter 3

Spring 1308 Eastern Bank of Lake Taheel

Placing a fur-wrapped parcel on the command table with a dull thud, Prince Althern sank into his chair. The flap of the tent rustled open, and Grand Marshal Pesus stooped through the entrance. Removing his fur-lined mittens, he cupped his hands and blew into them vigorously, his breath misting in the bitter air.

"You'd think, surrounded by a forest full of flammable trees, it wouldn't be this cold," Pesus grumbled.

Althern chuckled, leaning back in his chair. "You've a full belly and more furs than most people see in a lifetime, Pesus. Are you sure it's not just old age catching up with you?"

Pesus shot the Prince a mock-injured look. "If I'm old, Sire, then you're not far behind. Thirty-four summers puts me only four ahead of you!"

Althern laughed, shaking his head as he unfurled a campaign map across the table. His eyes flicked toward the tent's entrance, where a nervous figure lingered just beyond the flap.

"Soldier Pax, you may enter," Althern called.

Startled, Pax pushed into the tent, standing stiffly opposite the Prince. Though young, his face bore the marks of hardship: small scars cut across his cheekbones, and his hands were calloused. A curl of brown hair fell stubbornly across his eyes, but he ignored it, straightening to his full height.

"Tell me your story, Pax," Althern said, his tone curious but commanding. "How did you come to serve in my army with only a hunting knife and a gut full of determination?"

Pax hesitated, taking a deep breath, unaware that the other captains had entered the tent behind him.

"My home is Juntya, just west of Garhelm Forest," Pax began, his voice steady but subdued. "My parents work as blacksmiths. We supplied blades to the city until last spring, when a royal courier arrived to cancel the trade orders. My father wasn't told why—we'd supplied the King for decades—but we heard rumours that cheaper foreign blades were being imported. Since then, we've barely scraped by. My parents struggled to keep food on the table."

Althern gestured for him to continue. "You worked the forge with your father, I assume?"

"Yes, since I was old enough to wield a hammer," Pax replied. "But when things got bad, I decided to leave home. I thought I could lighten their burden—one less mouth to feed. I made for the only place I thought I could find work: the city of Epiris. On my first day, I met a recruiter."

The Prince's expression softened. "And your parents—they supported this decision?"

Pax's shoulders slumped slightly, and his face darkened with painful recollection. "I didn't tell them, Sire. That night, I heard them arguing over whether to kill our last chicken for food. I waited until they were asleep, then I slipped out with only my knife and the warmest clothes I had."

Althern's gaze lingered on the young soldier, his voice

gentler now. "Pax, I hope one day you return to your mother with enough coin to ease her worries. More importantly, return to her so she no longer has to relive the pain of your leaving, wondering why you left in silence. Your selflessness is clear—don't ever lose that."

Sliding the fur-wrapped parcel across the table, Althern gestured for Pax to open it.

Pax carefully unwrapped the furs, revealing a well-kept arming sword. Its black leather-bound handle was balanced and sturdy, and the scabbard bore intricate, decorative tracings. Next to it lay a pair of simple leather gauntlets, reinforced with scales on the knuckles and fingers.

Pax's breath caught as he slowly unsheathed the blade. The metallic rasp filled the tent as he turned it over in his hands with surprising skill. His eyes widened when he spotted the maker's mark near the hilt—a broad oak leaf stamped into the steel.

"This is my father's mark," Pax said, his voice filled with awe. "Sire, thank you for showing me this. But… how did you know?"

Althern clasped his hands together, a faint smile playing on his lips. "A happy coincidence, young Pax. This sword was one of my old training blades. The fact that your father forged it is nothing short of destiny. It served me well during my years of training, and now, I gift it to you. Who am I to stand in the way of such an alignment of the stars?"

Pax stared at the Prince, his mouth agape.

"I ask only one thing in return," Althern continued. "Strive to survive long enough to repay this debt. One day, introduce me to your father. I would thank him personally for his fine craftsmanship."

A tear slipped down Pax's cheek, splashing onto the dusty floor. Overcome with emotion, he sheathed the sword and bowed deeply. "Thank you, Sire," he managed, his voice thick.

Althern smiled. "Now, off with you. That blade hasn't been oiled or sharpened in ten years. You've work to do."

Pax nodded eagerly, clutching the sword and gauntlets to his chest as he exited the tent.

Pesus shook his head as he watched the boy leave. "Why do you give so much of yourself to them, Sire? He's a ranker. He could be dead by summer. Or worse, he might sneak off into the night and sell that blade for a quick profit at the traders' forum."

Althern leaned back in his chair, his gaze thoughtful. "Because, Pesus, now he has a reason to live. And because some clerk in my father's court robbed his family of their livelihood. That boy may not be a soldier yet, but with the right investment, he could go far."

Pesus frowned but said nothing more, following Althern's lead as the captains took their seats around the command table. To Althern's right sat Grand Marshal Pesus, Altherns second-in-command and the overseer of the army when the Prince was away. Beside him was Captain Ghoshte, the sinewy and sharp-eyed leader of the archers and hunters, perpetually covered in dirt from the field.

To the Prince's left sat Captain Felix, the leader of the knights. His pristine white surcoat and polished armour made him appear as regal as he was dangerous, his soft-spoken manner hiding the temperament of a coiled predator. Next to Felix was Captain Bones, a scarred and battle-hardened warrior who commanded the front rankers. Known for his bloodlust and gruff demeanour, Bones was a man who revelled in combat, earning his nickname from countless skirmishes.

"Thank you for joining me," Althern began. "I have

received word from the King regarding the state of the realm."

He gestured to the map spread across the table. "For years, traders passing through the lands of my brothers, Rok to the northeast and Asos to the southwest, have faced danger. Rok and his Brotherhood prey on caravans near the Spine Mountains, while Asos's hired thugs harass the southern roads. But now, reports are coming in of traders found dead within our borders. Villages to the east have gone silent. My father fears that my brothers may be laying the groundwork for something far more dangerous."

Pesus raised an eyebrow. "Rok and Asos? They lack the courage—or the organisation—for an invasion. They hate each other almost as much as they hate your father. They wouldn't work together."

"Unlikely, yes," Althern conceded. "But we owe it to our people to be certain. If they have crossed into our lands, or harmed our people, we must respond. Our orders are clear: we will patrol the eastern border, re-establish contact with the villages of Niborya and Taheel, and investigate the Borya Forest for signs of movement. I will take the cavalry and link up with Taheel, then catch up with the rest of you as you march to Niborya. At first light, we break camp and head east."

Pesus frowned. "Two hundred and thirty men aren't enough if there's an army waiting for us. Peacetime has softened many of them—they're untested."

Althern gave a faint smile. "Then let's hope we catch them sleeping." He glanced at Bones. "Besides, if we don't, I trust you'll make up for the shortfall."

Bones grunted, a ghost of a smile tugging at his scarred face.

The Prince rose, signalling the end of the meeting. As the captains filed out, Pesus lingered, his eyes fixed on the map.

"If Rok or Asos have breached the forest," he muttered, "we're in deep trouble."

Shaking his head, Pesus stepped outside into the biting morning air. The camp stirred around him, soldiers busying themselves with preparations for the march ahead. He sighed, muttering to himself, "Something tells me things won't stay the same for much longer."

Chapter 4

Spring 1308 Southeast of Lake Taheel

The camp buzzed with activity as the sun rose on a cool, damp morning. The scent of woodsmoke hung thick in the air, wafting from the various fires scattered throughout the encampment. Soldiers huddled around the flames, eating their breakfast and preparing for the day's journey. Whispers of the imminent departure had spread the previous night, likely started by an overly talkative guard stationed outside the command tent.

Prince Althern stood just outside the tent, chewing on a piece of salted meat, content to listen to the lively banter among his officers. The sound of Captain Bones and Captain Felix arguing drifted over to him, as familiar as it was entertaining.

"All I'm saying," Felix began, his voice dripping with mock patience, "is that if we're marching into villages, the people want to see polished armour and proper soldiers first. First impressions matter."

Bones bristled immediately, his broad shoulders stiffening. "We're front rankers. It's in the name, isn't it? We march from the front and fight at the front. And who are you calling unprofessional? Half my men could wipe the floor with your shiny tin soldiers."

Felix smirked, knowing he'd riled Bones up. "Careful, Captain. Don't work yourself into an early grave."

Before Bones's temper boiled over, Felix pivoted smoothly, turning his attention to the Prince. "You'll take care with that lot of cavalry, won't you, Sire? We'd hate to lose you to some nasty little ambush."

Althern grinned. "Of course, Felix. I have to make it back to look after the lot of you, don't I?"

Content that his officers were in good spirits, Althern excused himself and made his way toward the cavalry. The mounted unit, already assembled and ready to depart, stood near the edge of the camp. Gleaming armour and polished tack reflected the morning light, a picture of discipline and readiness.

Within the hour, Althern and his thirty mounted cavalry departed, heading north-west around the shores of Lake Taheel toward Taheel Village. The first leg of the journey was slow, the forest's ancient roots and fallen branches forcing them to keep to a cautious walk. The woodland pressed close on either side, its dense canopy casting shifting patterns of light and shadow across the ground.

By mid-morning, the forest thinned, giving way to a well-used traders' route that skirted the lake. Althern urged his men to pick up the pace, the horses settling into a steady trot. The mid-spring sun climbed higher, and the Prince wiped the sweat from his brow as his felt-lined helmet became sodden.

As they rounded a bend, Althern spotted a familiar sight, a fishing hut perched near the lake, its long wooden jetty flanked by several moored boats. He raised his voice above the rhythmic clatter of hooves. "We'll stop for water at the fishing hut."

The mounted soldiers murmured their acknowledgement, and the group slowed as they approached. Althern's sharp eyes caught movement—an old fisherman sat outside the hut, weaving a fishing net with practiced ease.

The Prince dismounted, handing his reins to one of his men, and approached the fisherman. "Good morning," he said warmly. "We don't mean to intrude. We just need to water the horses and perhaps ask you a few questions."

The fisherman didn't look up, his hands moving in a steady rhythm as he worked the net. For a moment, Althern wondered if the man was deaf.

Without lifting his eyes, the fisherman spoke, his voice slow and laced with venom. "Forgive me if I don't rise and bow, my Prince."

The words caught Althern off guard, but before he could respond, the man continued. "I have a little difficulty these days, thanks to you and your band of merry men."

The fisherman finally met Althern's gaze, flicking open his heavy wool robe to reveal his legs. Both were tightly bound with blood-soaked bandages, the fabric discoloured with a pale yellow stain in places.

Most royals would have bristled at such a hostile greeting, but Althern's expression darkened with concern. "One leg is an unfortunate accident. But two?"

The fisherman sucked in a sharp breath. "You've no idea, do you?" He shook his head, his anger building. "Your family swore to protect this land, but Taheel is gone—your protection failed us!"

Althern frowned deeply. "Gone? What happened?"

"Two days ago," the fisherman spat, "a band of soldiers from the east raided the village. They pillaged, burned, and killed. They weren't just bandits—they were organised. Three hundred men, at least. They moved like shadows through the forest, silent until they struck. Archers, foot soldiers, and their leader—a mounted man. They carried good equipment, armour, and bows. Scruffy, maybe, but far from ordinary thieves. I'd say they were men of the forest."

Althern's jaw tightened. The Forest Dwellers from Garhelm had rarely ventured so far south.

"What of the people? The King's retainers?"

The fisherman snorted bitterly. "The retainers awoke to the sound of fighting and were cut down before they could mount a defence. As for the villagers—" His voice faltered before hardening again. "They lined us up in the market square. Man, woman, and child. Anyone who moved or cried out was killed. Then their leader walked down the line, killing every other person. Bodies everywhere."

He gestured to his bandaged legs. "For those of us spared, they made sure we couldn't fight back. Their leader, the rider… he drove his sword through both my legs. Didn't even blink."

Althern clenched his fists, his mind racing. Taheel was a vital village, home to around a hundred people. Retired knights had been settled there to act as a deterrent, yet they'd been overwhelmed.

"How many survived?"

"Maybe forty," the fisherman said quietly. "But how can we rebuild after this? We don't even feel safe in our own beds anymore."

Althern signalled one of his men to replace the fisherman's bandages with fresh ones from their packs. "You've done well to hold on," Althern said softly. "We'll see to it that this is not forgotten."

The Prince spent a little more time speaking with the fisherman before bidding him farewell. As the party mounted up and rode on, the gravity of the situation weighed heavily on them.

It wasn't long before they crested a small rise, and the village of Taheel came into view. The sight stole the breath from Althern's chest.

Fires still smouldered in several places, their smoke curling into the sky like ghostly tendrils. Burnt-out buildings stood as skeletal remnants, their frames blackened and charred. The central traders' forum, once bustling with life, was eerily empty, its cleared ground littered with debris.

On the outskirts, homes that had once been filled with the laughter of children and the chatter of families were now silent. The devastation was absolute.

Althern sat motionless for a moment, his hands gripping the reins tightly. His men exchanged sombre glances, the weight of the scene pressing down on them all.

"We'll ride through," Althern said finally, his voice low but firm. "Keep your eyes open. We need to know exactly what we're dealing with."

As the party descended into the ruins of Taheel, the prince couldn't shake the gnawing dread in his chest. If this was only the beginning, what horrors awaited them further east?

Chapter 5

Spring 1308 Village of Taheel

Picking their way through the ruins of Taheel, Althern and his men manoeuvred their horses carefully to avoid stepping on the bodies that littered the streets. In the warmth of the spring sun, the unmistakable stench of decomposition hung thick in the air, forcing many to tie cloth rags over their faces.

A small group of villagers worked nearby, dragging corpses into piles around the market square. Black smoke billowed from already burning pyres, rising into the cloudless midday sky. The villagers barely glanced at the newcomers. Recognising the King's insignia on their armour, they returned to their grim task without pause.

Althern dismounted, handing his reins to one of his men. He turned to his deputy, his voice steady despite the carnage around them. "Take ten riders and scout the edges of the village. Ensure we're alone. Rotate guard patrols and send your fastest rider to warn Grand Marshal Pesus of what we've found. If these forest dwellers have made it this far west, they've already passed through Niborya. Pesus must know—we'll need to regroup with him at Juntya before it's too late."

As his deputy barked orders, Althern noticed a man among the villagers. He moved from person to person, offering bread and water, encouraging those who protested to take something. Despite his slim frame, his thick shoulders and scarred arms hinted at a life of hard service.

Althern strode toward him, motioning for his soldiers to stand down. As he approached, the man turned, his face streaked with ash and sweat. He stood slightly taller than the Prince, his bearing more military than villager.

"Sire," the man said, bowing slightly. "A welcome sight, though I fear you're a little late. Name's Daka. I served your father until my retirement last year."

Althern waved the gesture away. "No need to bow, Daka. I'm sorry this has happened to you and your people. Where's the mayor?"

Daka cast a glance over his shoulder at one of the smouldering pyres. "He's with the gods now," he said simply.

Althern grimaced, his eyes scanning the worn faces of the villagers who had turned to watch. "They look to you as their leader. What do you need?"

Daka surveyed the devastation around him, his gaze calculating. "We need to clear the streets before the pests come and bring disease with them. We'll need wood—plenty of it—for the pyres. But even then, Sire, it's not just the buildings that need rebuilding. The people do too. And that will take time."

Althern nodded grimly. Pulling his soldiers to one side, he issued a series of quick orders. Within moments, the men sprang into action.

The Prince's cavalry quickly unhitched their mounts and gathered carts from around the village square. Two soldiers were assigned to each cart, moving through the streets to load the bodies with as much dignity as possible. Meanwhile, others fanned out, searching for axes and tools among the ruined houses before heading into the nearby woodland to gather firewood.

Althern removed his armour, keeping only his sword at his belt, and joined the villagers in their work. Ignoring the rancid smell of decay, he dragged bodies toward the growing pyres.

Daka, watching the future King hauling corpses alongside his people, opened his mouth to speak but thought better of it. Instead, he joined Althern at the edge of a new pile, silently resuming his grim task.

Hours passed. By the time the last of the bodies were cleared from the streets, the pyres were roaring, filling the sky with thick columns of smoke. Daka leaned on a stick, pulling down the cloth mask from his face.

"I'd say that's most of it done, Sire," he said. "Those carts were a blessing. Without the horses, we'd have been at this for days."

Althern's once-white tunic was streaked with ash and grime. Taking a waterskin from his horse's saddlebag, he drank deeply before offering it to his returning deputy, who arrived with two mounted soldiers in tow.

"What did you find?" Althern asked.

The deputy wiped sweat from his brow before answering. "The tracks of a large group lead northwest, up to the forest's edge, but they vanish the moment they enter the woods. Either they're ghosts, or they're highly skilled at covering their movements. The tracks we did find are at least a day old."

Before Althern could reply, the sound of a bowstring snapping broke the uneasy quiet. One of the soldiers fell from his horse, an arrow buried in his throat. His body hit the ground with a sickening thud, blood pooling beneath him.

"Ambush!" Althern shouted, drawing his sword as chaos erupted around him. Villagers screamed and fled, the faint clinking of armour from the eastern side of the village signalling the approach of enemy forces.

Althern counted the men at his side—nine in total, including his deputy and Daka. The enemy foot soldiers emerged from the narrow streets moments later: ten men in scale armour, their gear a strange blend of expensive craftsmanship and the forest-dweller's ragged camouflage.

"Between the carts!" Althern ordered, rallying his men. "Use them to cover the flanks. Let's kill these bastards before their archer gets into position!"

The Prince's men formed a defensive line between the carts, their swords drawn. The enemy advanced silently, their movements eerily precise. At the last moment, Althern roared, his men echoing the cry as they clashed with the attackers in a violent collision of steel.

A slender enemy soldier lunged for Althern's neck, his blade flashing in the sunlight. Althern parried just in time, the force of the blow forcing him back a step. The bandit swung again in a wide arc, but Althern ducked, countering with a feint to the midriff. As the attacker moved to block, Althern drove his blade across the man's exposed throat. Blood sprayed as the soldier crumpled to the ground.

To his right, Daka dispatched an enemy with a brutal thrust to the stomach, already engaging another before the first had hit the dirt. Althern stepped forward, finishing off the groaning man with a quick stab to the chest.

A shout drew his attention to his left. His deputy was pinned against a cart, fending off a relentless assault with only a dagger. Althern moved quickly, driving his sword through the attacker's neck. The blade caught in the man's spine, but the force of the blow was enough to drop him.

As Althern turned, he realised the fighting had stopped. Bodies littered the square, his men standing bloodied but victorious.

"Check for survivors," Althern ordered. "If any are alive, I want answers before they meet their gods."

Daka wiped blood from his face with his sleeve. "Sorry, Sire," he said grimly. "They all died quick deaths."

Althern sighed. "Sound the retreat. I want all men back in this square, fully armoured, by sundown. We'll need a defensible position for the night. They must have been scouts or a hunting party fancying their chances"

As the deputy raised his horn and gave three sharp blasts, a faint whistling sound reached Althern's ears. His instincts screamed too late—something struck him in the back, the force sending him crashing to the ground.

He tasted dirt, his vision blurring as he tried to lift his head. Through the haze, he saw his deputy clutching at an arrow buried in his stomach, collapsing moments later. Althern tried to cry out, but no sound came.

The darkness closed in, swift and unforgiving, leaving the Prince still and motionless on the edge of the square.

Chapter 6

Spring 1308 Borya Forest

Grand Marshal Pesus had driven the men hard through the morning. Now, with the sun past its peak, he called a halt for a water break and to allow the soldiers to eat. The archer captain, Ghoshte, sent his men to form a perimeter around the weary column, setting a protective screen while the rest of the party rested.

From here, the forest thickened, the canopy promising to steal their sunlight and limit visibility. Pesus knew the terrain ahead would slow them even further. He planned to send the archers ahead to scout and reduce the risk of unpleasant surprises.

As Pesus surveyed the men, his attention was drawn to raised voices. Near the edge of the group, Captain Bones was gesticulating wildly at Captain Felix. It wasn't the first time those two had clashed today.

Sighing, Pesus strolled toward the commotion just in time to hear Felix's crisp, mocking tone.

"All I'm saying, Bones, is if your men could tread a little more carefully, we wouldn't be marching through a swamp of their own making. My knights don't need their armour caked in mud when we arrive at Niborya. First impressions matter, you know."

Bones's face darkened. "Tread lightly? We're on a bloody march, not a tea party! I'm surprised your men's tears haven't washed the mud away already. Get a grip!"

Without waiting for a response, Bones stormed past Pesus, snatching a chunk of bread from a soldier's ration and stuffing it into his mouth.

Felix, watching Bones retreat, smirked and turned to Pesus with a glint of mischief in his eye. "I think I might've wound him up a bit."

Pesus raised an eyebrow. "Keep at it, and his head might actually explode."

Felix laughed but shrugged, entirely unrepentant. "Perhaps I should stop. Eventually."

Pesus doubted he would. "How are your knights holding up with the extra weight?"

Felix gestured toward his unit. "They're managing fine for now. They've trained for this—long marches in full armour are routine. But once we hit the forest proper, it'll slow us down. Roots and uneven ground won't do the mules or men any favours."

Pesus nodded, noting the logic. "We'll adjust the pace. I'll have a word with Bones to keep the front rankers from getting too far ahead. I don't want the column stretched thin."

Felix tilted his head toward the sun, soaking in the warmth. "Best enjoy this while it lasts. It'll be cold under the canopy soon enough."

The column pushed on, entering the dense woodland by mid-afternoon. Progress slowed as roots and fallen branches threatened both riders and pack animals. Bones led the front rankers at a steady pace, his men carefully navigating the treacherous terrain.

As the sun began to dip below the horizon, Pesus called a halt. The captains gathered around him as he issued orders.

"The forest has slowed us more than I expected," Pesus admitted, glancing at the shadowy treetops. "We won't reach Niborya before nightfall. We'll camp here instead. Ghoshte, send your men hunting before we lose the light. Felix, your knights will take first watch. Bones, your front rankers are to build a barricade—use whatever you can find to secure the perimeter."

The captains nodded, their usual banter replaced with grim determination. As the soldiers set to work, the camp began to take shape.

Ghoshte and his archers slipped away, returning an hour later laden with rabbits and even a young deer. The sight lifted the men's spirits, and a hearty stew was soon simmering over the fires. Meanwhile, the knights had de-kitted and joined the effort to reinforce the barricades, while the front rankers rotated between sentry duty and gathering wood.

Pesus took a final walk around the camp, a bowl of rabbit stew in hand. The makeshift fortifications were as solid as they could be under the circumstances, and the men seemed as prepared as possible. As the fires burned low and soldiers settled in for the night, Pesus found a spot near the mules, pulled his fur cloak tight, and drifted into a restless sleep.

The first sign of trouble was the mules. They grew restless, stamping and pulling at their ties. Pesus stirred as one of the animals let out a panicked shriek, its cry abruptly silenced.

"Wolves!" came the cry from a sentry. "We're being attacked!"

Ghoshte was already on his feet, an arrow nocked and ready. The twang of his bowstring was followed by a yelp as his shot found its mark. Pesus leapt to his feet, drawing his sword and scanning the darkness for movement.

"Light the fires!" Felix bellowed, grabbing wood from the barricades and shouting for his men to do the same.

Pesus's eyes caught movement atop a fallen tree near the mules. Three grey wolves bounded over the log with fluid ease, followed by two more. They were heading straight for the front rankers, who had been asleep nearest the log. The men scrambled to form a rough semi-circle, but the sudden chaos blocked the archers' line of sight.

"Bones, pull your men back!" Pesus shouted, but his voice was lost in the confusion.

Bones, oblivious to the warning, stood firm in the centre of the semi-circle. A wolf seized the opportunity, leaping at him with a feral snarl. Its teeth sank deep into his forearm, its claws scraping harmlessly against his chest plate.

With a roar of rage, Bones tried to pry the wolf's jaws open but failed. Instead, he wrapped his free arm around the creature's ribs, crushing it against his broad chest. The wolf let out a pained whine before falling limp. Bones dropped it to the ground and turned to face the remaining wolves, daring them to attack.

"Bones! Get down!" Pesus yelled, dropping to the ground to emphasise his point.

Bones glanced at the Grand Marshal, confused for a moment, before realisation dawned. He and his men hit the dirt just as a volley of arrows whistled overhead. Each shot found its mark, and the wolves fell in a chorus of yelps.

The initial breach was over, but sporadic attacks continued through the night. Wolves darted in and out of the shadows, their glowing eyes briefly visible before disappearing into the darkness. The archers, hindered by poor visibility, loosed arrows at every opportunity, killing a few more.

By dawn, the attacks had ceased, and the camp was quiet. Pesus surveyed the aftermath: two front rankers had been killed during a breach on the opposite side of camp, and a knight had sustained a leg wound. Bones's arm was bandaged, but he seemed unbothered by the injury.

The centre of camp was littered with wolf carcasses, now being skinned by the archers. Despite the losses, Pesus considered it a lucky escape. "We'll move at first light," he told his captains, his tone firm. "The sooner we're out of this forest, the better."

As the sun rose, the men began to break camp, their faces tired but resolute. Pesus watched them with a quiet determination, knowing the challenges ahead would only grow harder.

Chapter 7

Spring 1308 Niborya Village

After a quick breakfast eaten in the grey light of dawn, the soldiers began assembling, ready to move. The air was tense; the forest around them seemed unnervingly still. Ghoshte and the other captains gathered with Grand Marshal Pesus near the command tent to plan their approach to Niborya.

Handing Captain Bones two bowls—one containing soup and the other a thick, pungent paste—Ghoshte said, "Here, drink this and rub the paste on your wound. It'll help prevent infection. Don't want you losing that arm, do we?"

Bones sniffed the paste and recoiled at its sharp, acrid smell. "Smells like death in a bowl."

"It's made from what I could forage," Ghoshte replied flatly, unimpressed by Bones's disdain. "Either you use it, or you lose the arm. Your choice."

Grumbling, Bones reluctantly applied the paste and wrapped his arm with fresh strips of fabric.

As the column advanced on Niborya, the morning sunlight filtered weakly through the dense forest canopy. Beams of golden light created an almost mystical atmosphere, though the eerie silence of the village quickly extinguished any sense of wonder. No chatter, no children's laughter, not even the crackle of a morning fire.

The first sign of what awaited them was the smell.

The stench of rotting flesh hit the front rankers first, and audible groans and retching echoed through the lines until the foul odour reached Pesus at the rear of the column.

"Silence your men," Pesus barked at his captains, his voice low and sharp. "This could still be a trap."

A strained quiet settled over the soldiers once more as they pressed on.

Pesus had sent Ghoshte and his archers ahead earlier to approach the village from the far side, ensuring there would be no escape for any remaining enemy forces. But as the front rankers reached the outskirts of the village, it became clear there was little chance of resistance.

The soldiers passed the first bodies scattered along the path. Some could not stop themselves from vomiting into the undergrowth. Men, women, children—all lay among the ruins. Many had been partially eaten by scavengers, but it was evident the villagers had died at the hands of men.

In the centre of the village, Pesus halted, surveying the grisly scene. The remains of a woman lay at his feet, her body twisted unnaturally.

From a nearby hut, Ghoshte emerged, his expression grim. He nodded a sombre greeting to the Grand Marshal before kneeling to inspect the corpse.

"This was the work of men," Ghoshte said quietly, pointing to a splintered rib bone. "Look here—chipped where a blade struck. The wolves came after, scavenging, but these people were already dead."

Pesus's jaw tightened as he scanned the desolation around them. The buildings had been stripped bare, any valuables or provisions taken. This wasn't just murder; it was calculated destruction.

"We don't have time to bury them," Pesus said eventually. "Gather oil and wood. We'll build pyres and give them to the gods. It's the least we can do."

Ghoshte hesitated, stepping closer to speak softly. "Marshal, the men who did this are already two, maybe three days ahead of us. The tracks lead toward Taheel. If we stop here to build pyres, we'll lose more time."

Pesus turned, his face set with grim determination. "We've already failed these people once. I won't leave them here to be picked apart by wolves and crows. We'll do this quickly."

While the front rankers began felling trees to fuel the pyres, Bones moved among his men, doing what he could to assist despite his injured arm. As he neared the forest's edge, a flicker of movement in the undergrowth caught his attention.

Drawing his blade, he advanced cautiously, the sounds of snapping branches underfoot betraying his every step. Twenty paces ahead, the shadow moved again, deliberate and purposeful.

Then it struck.

With a burst of speed, a massive grey wolf leapt from the undergrowth, claws outstretched and teeth bared. Bones barely managed to get his free hand around the beast's throat, holding its snapping jaws just far enough away from his face. The weight of the creature drove him to the ground, knocking the wind from him.

His sword fell uselessly from his grasp as the wolf's claws scraped at his chest plate. Bones gritted his teeth, his muscles burning as he fought to keep the animal's fangs from finding his neck.

The wolf was old, its face and shoulders scarred from countless battles. Its hot breath reeked of decay, and Bones's vision began to blur as his strength waned.

Just as he thought he was finished, a powerful yelp broke through the struggle. The weight on his chest vanished as the wolf was thrown aside.

Struggling to sit up, Bones stared in stunned silence. Towering over the grey wolf was a magnificent white wolf, nearly twice its size, its coat glowing faintly in the dim light. The grey wolf, now cowering on its back, bared its belly in submission. The white wolf sniffed at it briefly before turning its attention to Bones.

Its piercing white eyes locked onto his, and despite its size and power, Bones felt no fear. Then, to his astonishment, a voice filled the air—a woman's voice, resonant and commanding, yet calm.

"You will not join your ancestors today, Captain Bones," the voice said, as if echoing inside his very mind. "Your path is not yet complete. When the time comes, you will meet a boy. Give him this—it is his by right."

The white wolf dipped its head, shaking loose a silver necklace, which slid over its fur and landed at Bones's feet. Without another glance, it padded silently into the forest, its glowing form fading into the shadows.

Bones sat frozen, his hands trembling as he picked up the necklace. A large white stone, shaped like a teardrop, hung from the silver chain. He slipped it into his pocket and, still dazed, stumbled back toward the village.

When Bones returned, the pyres were nearly complete. Pesus and the other captains stood in the village centre, supervising the final preparations.

Pesus spotted Bones's pale face and furrowed his brow. "What's wrong with you? You look like you've seen a ghost."

Bones rubbed his hands together, avoiding Pesus's gaze. "What the hell was in that stew you gave me this morning, Ghoshte?"

Ghoshte frowned. "Rabbit, some vegetables from the mule packs, and foraged mushrooms. Why?"

Bones grunted and poured water from his skin over his face. "Explains it."

He offered no further explanation, and the other captains decided not to press him.

By midday, the pyres were burning, thick smoke rising into the sky as the villagers were sent to their gods. Pesus gave the order to move, the column retracing their steps westward toward Taheel.

The march was uneventful, and by the time the sun dipped below the horizon, they had cleared the forest and made camp on its outskirts. Tomorrow, they would reach Taheel.

Pesus stood watch as the camp settled for the night, the weight of the day's horrors pressing heavily on his shoulders. He could only hope the next village would still stand when they arrived.

Chapter 8

Spring 1308 Taheel Village

Somewhere nearby, food was cooking. The hiss and crackle of a fire reached Althern's ears, and the smell of roasting meat made his stomach rumble. Slowly, he opened one eye and saw nothing but the rough roof of a hut. The last thing he remembered was seeing his deputy take an arrow before everything went black.

Althern tried to prop himself up on his elbows for a better view, but a searing pain erupted in his left shoulder, stealing his breath. He dropped back onto the bed, gasping. An uncomfortable lump of material was packed into a bandage around his back and shoulder. He must have made a racket, for the door creaked open, and Daka stepped inside carrying a steaming bowl of stew.

"Here, get some of this down you," Daka said, his voice firm but kind. "Your body's in shock."

Daka helped Althern sit up slowly, careful to avoid aggravating the injury. Grimacing at the discomfort, the prince nodded his thanks and took the bowl.

"What happened?" Althern rasped. "What of my deputy?"

Daka paced the room as he explained the events that had unfolded after the prince was struck down.

"After you went down, none of us knew if you were alive or dead. The men formed a shield circle around your body, but the arrows kept coming from the shadows. It was clear it was only one archer—the same one from before, we think. We finally got eyes on him, he was lying flat on the roof of a house at the edge of the square. I readied a group to circle around and flush him out, but before we could move, he stood to take another shot."

Daka paused, shaking his head at the memory. "He never hit his mark. The bastard went limp and fell backwards off the roof. When we reached him, we found an arrow sticking out of his chest—white feathers, with a smudge of red. We searched high and low for another archer, but there was no one. It made no sense."

Althern frowned, his mind clouded by the strange details.

"It didn't stop there," Daka continued. "The lads cutting wood in the forest turned up not long after, having heard the deputy's horn. But they didn't come alone—they brought a girl with them, bedraggled-looking thing. Says her name is Arla, but she hasn't spoken a word to anyone. We even had some of the village women try to coax her, but nothing. The odd thing is, she had a quiver of arrows— white feathers with red smudges, just like the one that killed the archer. No bow, though. Someone out there is protecting her."

Althern absorbed the puzzling account, nodding for Daka to go on.

"Your deputy didn't make it," Daka said, his voice lowering. "The arrow punctured his organs. I had to put him out of his misery—there was no saving him. As for you, the arrow glanced off your shoulder bone. It'll hurt like hell for a while, but you'll live. We dressed the wound with honey and herbs to stave off infection."

Althern opened his mouth to reply, but exhaustion overwhelmed him. His head fell back against the pillow, and darkness consumed him once more.

Daka watched the prince slip back into unconsciousness, concern etching deep lines into his face. He really did look like his father. The veteran draped a deer hide over Althern and stepped out into the cool night air.

Of the thirty men who had arrived at Taheel, five were wounded, two sent as messengers, and three dead, including the deputy. That left twenty men to defend the village and the prince until reinforcements arrived.

Gathering the remaining men around the fire, Daka addressed them. "I need a volunteer party for a scouting mission. Two objectives: first, ensure no one's sneaking up on us in the dark. Second, locate the bows those soldiers buried or hid nearby. They clearly weren't infantrymen looking at them, their bows are worth more to them than their lives, the forest dwellers from the east. If we're attacked again, we'll need every advantage."

The prince's bodyguards—elite soldiers handpicked from the King's own ranks—rose to their feet before Daka had finished speaking. Their loyalty to Althern was unwavering.

"Eager lot, aren't you?" Daka chuckled, scanning the group. "Alright, you four—and you four."

Toward the front, a younger soldier raised his hand. "Sir, I'd like to come on the patrol. I haven't served as long as the others, but I want to prove myself."

Daka studied the soldier for a moment before giving a small smile. "Stand on your left leg until I say stop."

Confused but determined, the soldier obeyed. At first, he stood still, staring straight ahead. Then, after a few seconds, his leg began to tremble. He dropped his foot to the ground, clutching his shin.

"How did you know?" the soldier asked, unstrapping his shin guard to reveal a shallow arrow wound oozing blood.

Daka blinked in mock offence. "I served twenty summers in the King's army, lad. I know when one of my men is injured. Besides, I saw you drop during the infantry charge earlier."

The veteran softened his tone. "But I've got a more important job for you anyway. Go sit with the prince. Reapply the ointment and change the bandage every hour. That's your assignment tonight."

The soldier's face lit up with pride as he limped off toward the hut.

Daka and his selected men prepared for the mission. "Nothing shiny, nothing that clinks or rattles," he instructed. "If it can't be dulled or bound in fabric, leave it behind."

Slipping back into a military role felt as natural to Daka as breathing. It hadn't been long since he'd left the King's Guard—the elite fighters handpicked from the ranks of knights to serve as the King's personal protectors. For five summers, he had stood among them, his skills honed to razor-sharp precision. Those years in the Hall were a stark contrast to the many seasons he'd spent before that, far from the polished stone of Epiris, battling on the untamed frontiers. There had always been conflict to get stuck into, especially since King Apius's two other sons had rebelled and claimed kingdoms of their own. The borders were a dangerous place to be with hired men lurking in the forests and mountains. Daka knew all too well the hardships of battle.

The rhythms of war were etched into him, an unshakable instinct. He knew how to command, how to fight, and how to endure. Yet, there was something different now, a faint pull at the edges of his thoughts. The years in the Guard had given him discipline, but the frontiers had taught him survival—a raw, primal edge that couldn't be dulled by palace walls. As he settled into the familiar patterns of military life once again, he found himself wondering if he'd ever truly left it behind. Or if it had simply lain dormant, waiting for the call.

Once ready, the party moved silently into the forest, the faint starlight barely illuminating their path. They headed toward a massive oak tree Daka remembered was a popular spot for children to play and climb. It seemed the most likely place the enemy had used for observation and concealment.

As they approached the oak, Daka dropped to one knee and signalled for his men to halt. Listening intently, he heard nothing but the faint rustle of leaves.

"Stay here," he whispered. "I'll take a look."

Creeping toward the massive root system, now suspended in the air, Daka examined the ground for signs of disturbance. Nothing obvious. He peered around the tree but saw no movement.

Suddenly, a faint, gritty sensation tickled his nostrils. He fought the urge to sneeze but froze when a voice, no more than a whisper, broke the silence.

"Hands up. Slowly."

Daka's heart pounded as he looked up to see a hooded figure perched in the roots above him. The tensioned wood of a nocked bow creaked faintly.

"I've an arrow laced with poison," the voice continued. "It'll pierce that leather vest and come out your back before you blink."

Daka slowly raised his hands, cursing his lapse in awareness. As a thin shaft of light fell across the figure's face, he realised he wasn't looking at a hardened warrior. The archer was a boy—no more than sixteen.

The boy's eyes darted toward a distant sound—one of Daka's men calling out. Seizing the distraction, Daka lunged at the boy's leg, throwing off his balance. The arrow loosed, its barb slicing across Daka's arm before burying itself harmlessly in the ground.

The boy thrashed and kicked, his boot connecting with Daka's nose with a sickening crunch. Blood poured down the veteran's face, but he held tight, dragging the boy to the ground and binding his hands and feet.

Daka's men arrived moments later, stunned by the sight of their furious leader holding down a struggling teenager.

"Get him up," Daka growled, wiping blood from his face. "And grab those bows."

He kicked at a bag scattered across the floor where the boy had been lay, it must have come loose during the scuffle.

"If the whole forest didn't already know we're here, they do now."

Chapter 9

Spring 1308 Taheel Village

The next morning, Daka was woken earlier than he'd have liked by one of the cavalrymen, who reported that a rider had returned from linking up with the Grand Marshal. By mid-morning, the rest of the Prince's army would arrive at Taheel.

Stiff and sore, Daka stretched, feeling the sting in his arm where the arrow had sliced it the day before. Luckily for him the poison had been a ruse and the boy admitted he hadn't laced the arrow with anything. He walked to the bucket at the end of his cot and splashed his face, trying to shake off the lingering grogginess.

"Oh, you've got to be kidding me," he muttered, catching sight of his reflection in the water. Overnight, he'd developed a spectacular black eye, a souvenir from his scuffle with the feral boy.

Back at the camp, the boy had been stripped of his weapons and placed under guard in the stable with the girl. Daka had planned to speak with them both that morning, but the imminent arrival of the main army quickly pushed the thought from his mind.

Pulling on a rough woollen tunic and strapping on his sword, the veteran stepped outside into the early light, heading toward the hut where Althern was being treated.

Inside, the injured soldier from the previous night was carefully rewrapping the prince's bandages, as instructed.

"Morning. How is he?" Daka asked.

The soldier frowned. "He's been asleep the whole time. Mumbling and groaning mostly. He was sweating through the night, even when it got cold. I think his blood's infected."

Daka's expression darkened. If Althern's wound had turned septic, his chances of survival were slim without a proper healer. Taheel's healer had been killed in the raid, and the nearest alternative was in Juntya—assuming the village hadn't already suffered the same fate. Aside from that, Daka had an old friend Marya who sometimes treated soldiers for him but she didn't like too many visitors. Her hut was in a remote part of Garhelm Forest, far away from civilisation.

Muttering a prayer under his breath, Daka stepped back into the square, where the morning sun had begun to break through the lingering mist. He called for the men who weren't on guard duty to assemble.

As they formed neat rows, Daka studied them. They looked worn and hungry, their faces gaunt from the gruelling days since arriving in Taheel. Making a mental note to send a hunting party eastward toward the lake where it was safer, he stepped forward to address them.

"Yes, before you ask," he began with a wry grin, "I do have a black eye from fighting a child. At least I won. I think."

The men laughed, some of the tension lifting from their shoulders.

"You'll be pleased to know the rest of your boys will

arrive just in time for dinner. But before that, we need to prepare the village for their arrival and feed you lot properly for once. Now, where are those bows we recovered last night?"

One of the soldiers led Daka to the blacksmith's workshop, or what was left of it. The building had been badly burned during the raid, but inside, the bows were laid out neatly on a bench.

"We cleaned them first thing this morning, Sir," the soldier explained. "They're incredible—nothing like I've seen before. Two pieces of wood bound together, and the draw is powerful."

Daka picked one up, running his hand along its polished surface. Each bow bore unique painted decorations, intricate and precise.

"I've seen this craftsmanship before," he murmured. "In Ghober Wood. That's Brotherhood territory… Surely, they wouldn't venture into Valhelm's lands."

There were eight bows in total. Daka selected eight of his hungriest-looking men and sent them out hunting, reasoning that their empty stomachs would make them all the more determined to catch something.

Before he could grab breakfast himself, the sentries sounded an alert from the eastern side of the village. The rest of the army, led by Grand Marshal Pesus, had arrived.

Pesus wasted no time upon his arrival. After a brief introduction to Daka, the Grand Marshal went straight to check on Althern. The prince lay pale and motionless, his forehead damp with sweat as the infection tightened its grip on his body.

Pesus dispatched riders to Epiris with urgent news for the King: his son's grave condition, the discovery of an enemy warband pillaging his lands, and the dire need for reinforcements.

The village bustled with activity as soldiers temporarily moved into the vacant homes and helped the locals repair the worst of the damage. Meanwhile, Daka led Pesus and the captains to his hut, providing them with food and wine before excusing himself to leave the leaders to their planning.

Remembering the boy in the stable, Daka made his way there, only to find the feral boy and his sister huddled in the straw, laughing uncontrollably. The boy was mimicking a dramatic kick before collapsing onto the floor, his tongue sticking out. Daka had no doubt who was being mocked.

The moment the boy noticed Daka, his laughter vanished. He stepped protectively in front of the girl and stared at the older man, waiting for him to speak.

"First off, I need to know who you are and where you're from," Daka said. "Because right now, you look a lot like a spy to me."

The boy shook his head. "I'm Casius. This is Arla, my sister. We're from Niborya, to the east."

Daka raised an eyebrow. "The Prince's army just came through Niborya—"

"They're too late," Casius interrupted. "Those men already passed through my village. They killed our mother. It's just us now. They passed by us at Lake Taheel only a day or so ago."

The boy's words silenced Daka for a moment. Finally, he asked, "So you saw the prince fall? You were watching us during the attack yesterday?"

Casius hesitated, then nodded.

"And it was you who shot the archer? The white-feathered arrow?"

The boy shrugged. "Yeah. I told Arla to wait by the forest, but then you lot captured her." He hesitated again before bowing his head. "Sorry about your face, mister. I didn't know if you'd hurt her or not."

Daka chuckled despite himself, the boy's honesty disarming him. "So, what's your plan now? Do you have any family to go to?"

"No," Casius admitted. "Our father died years ago, and with our mother gone, it's just us. I swore I'd get revenge on the man who killed her. That's all I have."

"And after you get your revenge? What then?"

The boy's silence spoke volumes.

Daka sighed. "Let me speak with Pesus. I may have a way for you to get your revenge—and live to care for your sister."

Later, in the command hut, Pesus debriefed Daka on the situation and surprised him with a proposition.

"Daka, you took charge when the Prince was incapacitated, and you've done an excellent job. The soldiers have spoken highly of you, and the knights who served with you in the past vouch for your skills. Myself and the other captains agree: we'd like to offer you a temporary captaincy within the army."

Daka's cheeks flushed, but he grinned. "I think I've got one more adventure in me Grand Marshal. What unit?"

"You'll command the knights," Pesus said, smiling. "Felix will take the cavalry."

By the time the hunting party returned, Daka had officially rejoined the King's army. The hunters brought back a haul of deer, rabbits, and even some fish from Lake Taheel. Ghosht inspected the kills with a critical eye, muttering disapproval at the unclean wounds.

Daka, however, clapped the hunters on the back. "Good

work, lads. Now let's see Ghosht and his archers put those recovered bows to proper use against the enemy!"

As the men laughed, Daka allowed himself a rare moment of satisfaction. He had returned to the fold—and he was ready for whatever came next.

Chapter 10

Spring 1308 Taheel Village

The guards changed a little before dawn, and Casius found himself restless. Days of trekking through the forest had given him purpose, but now, confined to the stable, he felt like a caged animal. The new guard, younger and with fewer scars than his predecessor, brought them bowls of leftover deer and vegetable broth from the night before. Casius accepted the two bowls gratefully, wolfing down his portion in record time.

The soldier noticed his hunger and tore off a piece of bread, passing it through the gate.

"Here, have some of this. You must be starving after days in the forest. What did you even eat out there?"

Casius explained how his father, a master hunter when he was alive, had taught him bits of hunting but they had to resort to berries and plants because of the pursuing bandits.

"I'm sorry about your mother," the soldier said softly. "My name's Pax. I'm new here too."

Casius noted Pax's easy manner and estimated there were only a few summers between them. The two chatted for nearly an hour, the soldier asking questions about the forest,

Casius's survival skills, and his journey. Arla stirred from her sleep, joining in briefly before boredom drove her back to her straw cot.

For the first time since his mother's murder, Casius felt a glimmer of normality. Since fleeing Niborya, he and Arla had survived the harsh terrain of Borya Forest, relying on intuition and luck. They had been shadowed by the band responsible for his mothers death until they had hidden in the forest whilst the bandits set upon Taheel. He cursed himself for being powerless when the screams and chaos erupted at the settlement. Against three hundred men, there was nothing he could do.

When the Prince's party had arrived at Taheel, Casius initially planned to move on, but something urged him to stay. Now, confined to the stable with little hope of catching up to the enemy, he felt the weight of frustration settling on his shoulders.

With Althern's condition worsening, Pesus mobilised the army to leave Taheel. A cart was loaded with straw and hides to transport the stricken heir, and Daka was summoned by the Grand Marshal.

"Morning, Captain," Pesus began. "We need to address the issue of your two captives. What will you do with them? I dare say they'll become a liability on the road."

Daka had mulled this over during the night. "The boy's a fighter," he replied. "Knows his way around a bow, and I could use an assistant. You know, with my age limitations."

Pesus allowed himself a small smile. "What of the girl? The army's no place for a young child."

"I agree," Daka nodded. "There's a healer where we can take the Prince—an old friend of mine. She's highly skilled and owes me a few favours. I'm hoping she'll take the girl in for a while, at least until Casius can figure things out himself."

Pesus arched an eyebrow. "Casius?"

"That's the boy's name," Daka confirmed. "I'll go and let him know the good news."

As Daka approached the stable, he noticed the guard was absent. The laughter echoing from within gave him a clue as to where he might be. He found Casius sitting on an upturned log, chatting animatedly with a front ranker.

For a moment, Daka considered reprimanding the soldier for being overly relaxed with a prisoner, but he decided against it. Instead, he called out to the boy.

"Casius, as we leave for Garhelm Forest today, I've a decision for you to make."

The boy cocked his head, his expression curious.

"As of now, you and your sister are free to go. You are no enemy of ours, and in fact, you most likely saved my men's lives by taking out that archer on the rooftops. For that, I am grateful. I have a way I can repay the favour—if you'll humour me."

Casius's head tilted further, almost animal-like.

"I'm taking on the captaincy of the Knights," Daka explained. "I'll need an assistant. Someone to fetch and carry my bags, run errands, clean my armour. You'd be paid the same as a front ranker. In return, I'll train you to fight with a sword and teach you to ride. You'll keep your bow—it's clear you already know how to use it. You might even be able to work with Ghoshte and the archers"

Casius's eyes narrowed. "What about Arla? Can she come too?"

Daka's face softened. "The army's no place for her. It's too dangerous, and she wouldn't keep up with the marches ahead of us. But I've a plan. We're taking the Prince to a healer in Garhelm Forest. Her name's Marya, she's knowledgable and could teach Arla. If anyone can keep her safe, it's Marya. With Valhelm in chaos, I'd want her somewhere deep in the forest, far from danger."

Casius glanced at his sister. She seemed interested, but the boy hesitated, torn between his desire for revenge and his sister's safety.

"I know it's a lot to trust," Daka said gently. "Take your time and think it over."

He excused himself, leaving the siblings alone in the stable.

Back in his hut, Daka sat heavily on his cot, the aches in his feet and back reminding him of the toll the last few days had taken. He rubbed his temples and chuckled softly. His life had taken an unexpected turn, but he welcomed it. After all, what was a soldier without a battle to fight?

He wondered about Casius. The boy had fire in him, no doubt, but could he temper that fire into something useful? Only time would tell. With a wry smile, Daka lay back on the cot, allowing himself a brief moment of rest before the march began.

CHAPTER 11

SPRING 1308 NORTH OF TAHEEL VILLAGE, GARHELM FOREST

As the front of the column snaked out of Taheel, the sharp blast of a horn from the rear signalled an approach. Grand Marshal Pesus immediately ordered the column to continue moving, then gathered Captain Felix and his cavalrymen to investigate. Riding swiftly to the source of the warning, Pesus was relieved to see a group of mounted men bearing the banner of Epiris galloping towards him.

"Well, I didn't expect reinforcements so soon" Pesus greeted them. "What brings you out here?"

One of the cavalrymen stepped forward to answer.

"When the King received the message about Prince Althern's condition, he dispatched fifty of us to reinforce your army."

Pesus nodded, the King's intent clear—he wanted this band of marauders dealt with decisively.

"I'm grateful for your assistance," Pesus said, gesturing to Captain Felix. "This is your commanding officer. For now, the front of the column is leaving the village, and we're heading into Garhelm Forest. Get yourselves settled."

As Pesus rode back to the head of the column, Felix took charge of the newcomers.

"Right, lads, feed and water your horses in the village while the rest of the column sorts itself out. You'll form the rearguard. The rest of you—split into groups and scout ahead."

By midday, the army was well underway. Reports came in of two-day-old tracks and signs that the enemy band had indeed passed this way. Riding with Daka and Bones along the well-worn trade route, Pesus noted the advantage of the terrain.

"This is a luxury we won't have for long," he said, gesturing to the clear ground around them. "If the band turns east, the terrain will thicken with trees and thorny undergrowth, forcing us to rely on the archers. If they've gone northwest..." He paused grimly. "I pray for Juntya."

Daka and Bones nodded silently. Bones, usually bickering with Captain Felix over trivial matters by this point in the march, seemed uncharacteristically subdued. Whether it was the arrival of reinforcements or the gravity of the situation, Pesus welcomed the peace.

Further ahead, Felix and ten cavalrymen were screening the forest before the main column arrived. The path remained quiet—too quiet. This was a well-used trade route, and Felix would have expected to encounter at least one caravan by now. Eventually, a dip in the landscape revealed signs of a recent camp. Cooking fires, now cold and scattered, dotted the clearing below. Felix raised a hand, halting his men, before cautiously leading them down into the hollow.

He dismounted at one of the extinguished fires, crouching to inspect the ashes. Spreading his hand over the coals, he noted a faint warmth lingering in the charred remains.

"Over a day old," he muttered to himself. Nearby,

discarded animal bones confirmed that a sizable force—likely three hundred strong—had camped here.

As Felix turned to mount his horse, a cry of disgust broke the stillness. Sword drawn, he rushed toward the source, only to find one of his men standing on one leg, cursing loudly. A foul-smelling brown slurry was slowly sliding down the soldier's lower calf.

"The filthy bastards!" the soldier snarled, glaring at what was clearly the band's makeshift latrine, now mixed into a pungent slurry by the rain.

Felix sheathed his sword, suppressing a grin as the other cavalrymen burst into laughter. Deciding not to add to the man's embarrassment, Felix remounted and led the group back to the track.

Not long after, the mood shifted. A scout from another group returned with news: a caravan had been spotted ahead. Suspecting a potential ambush, Felix called a halt to the column and summoned Captain Ghosht and his archers.

Ghosht split his men into two groups, slipping silently into the trees on either side of the track. Meanwhile, Felix positioned his cavalry in a shield wall, advancing cautiously toward the caravan.

As they neared, Felix noticed something odd.

"The horses," one of his men pointed out. "They're missing."

Felix frowned. A caravan this size should have been pulled by two strong horses, but none were in sight. He called out a challenge, his voice echoing through the trees. No response came.

He spurred his horse forward, halting ten paces from the caravan. What he saw made his stomach turn.

The figure standing by the caravan was no longer alive. He had been impaled lengthwise on a stake driven into the ground, the point entering through his groin and exiting through his mouth, forcing his jaw open. Birds had already begun picking at the soft flesh of his face, and his eyes were gone.

Felix dismounted, his gaze shifting to the caravan itself. Across the driver's seat lay the body of a young girl, no older than seven summers. Her pale, broken body was a grotesque sight, a stark reminder of the enemy's cruelty.

Ghoshte emerged silently from the trees, placing a hand on Felix's shoulder. "The caravan's been ransacked. Looks like a general trader. We should get this out of sight before the rest of the column arrives."

With solemn efficiency, the men dismantled the cart, using its wood to build a pyre. Felix guessed the man and girl had been father and daughter; either way, they would meet their gods together. As the pyre burned, the column passed by, soldiers craning their necks to glimpse the grim scene.

Felix and Ghoshte returned to their positions at the head of the column, their thoughts heavy. Whoever led this enemy band was ruthless. Even in war, women and children were usually spared. Not this time.

A couple of hours before sundown, the column reached a clearing near a spring. Pesus called a halt, ordering the men to set up camp and secure the area.

In the centre of the clearing, the captains convened. Pesus dismounted, stretching his back with a groan.

"Daka," he said, turning to the veteran. "The healer's hut is east of here, yes? Before we turn west toward Juntya?"

Daka nodded.

"Good. Take the Prince, the girl, and his original bodyguard. Leave the reinforcements with us. Stay there for the night, then rejoin us by midday tomorrow. Take care, old man. I need you back in one piece."

The veteran smiled grimly, summoning Casius and Arla. As the cavalrymen prepared the Prince for departure, Daka studied Althern's pallid face. The heir had woken a few times during the day, but he was feverish, disoriented, and barely coherent. His skin was clammy, his hands cold. Daka feared the infection might already be too far gone.

Mounting his horse, he muttered a prayer under his breath. For the Prince. For Arla. For them all. Then, with a final glance at Pesus, he led the small group eastward into the forest.

Chapter 12

Spring 1308 Garhelm Forest

As the light faded behind the treeline, Daka urged his men onward. Mounted and moving deeper into the forest, he kept a watchful eye on their surroundings. He had made this journey many times before, but not in the dark. The woods could turn into a maze once the last rays of sunlight disappeared, and he didn't want to risk losing the path.

He was searching for a stone dais, an ancient relic once used by the old inhabitants of these lands for sacrifices and religious rites. When he found it, he knew to turn right and follow the narrow path for five hundred paces to reach Marya's cabin.

The forest grew darker with every passing moment, and Daka found himself doubting his vision. Perhaps it was his age, or perhaps he wasn't concentrating. Either way, the dais seemed to appear from nowhere, almost under his horse's hooves. He reined in sharply, muttered a curse under his breath, and turned his mount down what appeared to be an animal track.

The forest was quiet, save for the soft snorts of the horses and the occasional rustling of leaves in the cool evening breeze. The stillness was broken by a voice ahead, calm yet commanding.

"You've brought company this time, Daka. Should I consider myself invaded?"

The words seemed to puncture the darkness. Daka's horse spooked momentarily before settling as Marya stepped from the shadows, her hand reaching to stroke the animal's nose. Her dark green felt cloak had camouflaged her among the trees, and her long black hair tumbled freely down her back.

"Marya," Daka said, inclining his head, "forgive the intrusion, especially at this hour. We've been on the road all day."

She didn't reply, merely turned and walked briskly down the track, beckoning him to follow with a flick of her head.

The cabin soon came into view, nestled in a clearing where thick vegetation carpeted the ground. The moonlight revealed a pond and a well near the main hut, while several outbuildings loomed in the shadows. Daka's men dismounted, letting their horses graze on patches of grass. At the rear of the group, the Prince's cart creaked to a halt. Althern, oblivious to the world around him, lay on the straw bed, his breathing shallow.

"I see you've been dragged back into a uniform," Marya observed, glancing at Daka as she stopped a few paces from him. Her expression carried a faint trace of disapproval.

"Temporarily," Daka replied, stepping closer. "Taheel's been attacked. There's a band from the east somewhere in these woods. It's dangerous times, Marya."

Her eyes narrowed. "Exactly what worries me," she said. "What is it you need? I assume this isn't a social visit."

Daka shifted uncomfortably. He hadn't visited Marya in years, not since her adopted mother had passed, and guilt weighed on him. "I apologise for that," he admitted. "But the

Prince needs your help. He's taken an arrow to the back, and the wound is badly infected. He's been out of it for days. I also have a favour to ask of you…"

"And the favour?" she asked, raising an eyebrow.

Daka nodded toward the cart. "That, too," he said.

Marya's gaze followed his, and her expression turned serious as she approached the cart. She placed a hand on the Prince's forehead, then unbuttoned his shirt to feel his chest with the back of her hand. Her tone turned sharp as she barked orders at the nearest soldiers.

"You, you, and you—carry him into the hut with the light in the window. Lay him on the table and strip him to the waist. The rest of you, clear out. Take your horses down the trail to the clearing past the dais and make camp. Move!"

When she turned to Daka, her voice was brisk. "I assume you're staying the night?"

"Yes," Daka replied. "But the men are the Prince's bodyguard. They shouldn't stray too far from him."

Marya rolled her eyes. Reaching out, she grabbed the reins of a nearby horse, yanking its head away from the foliage it had been chewing. Leaning in close to the soldier holding the reins, she spoke low but with a bite.

"Your horse is now fatally poisoned. Those leaves it's been eating are from a Popkin plant. Lethal to animals and humans alike. Fortunately for you, when boiled, they also make an antidote. Where you're standing is my garden, so if you value your horses, move them—and yourselves—down the track as instructed. Or do soldiers no longer follow orders?"

Without waiting for a reply, she strode off toward one of the outbuildings, lighting a lamp and gathering supplies. The soldiers, stunned into silence, needed no further encouragement. They mounted up and moved toward the clearing, muttering apologies as they went.

Inside the hut, the light from the lamps revealed bundles of drying herbs and plants hanging from the ceiling. Marya bustled in behind the soldiers carrying the Prince, her arms full of jars and vials.

"If you think you know what something is, you don't," she snapped at Daka. "Don't touch anything. Don't move anything. In fact, keep your hands to yourself."

She worked quickly, checking Althern's pulse, inspecting his wound, and muttering under her breath. The flesh around the arrow wound had darkened, and a foul smell lingered in the air.

"This was an arrow wound?" she asked. "Did you recover the arrow?"

Daka shook his head. "It was burned after it was removed."

Marya placed her hands on her hips, her sharp tone softening slightly as she glanced at him. "This is serious, Daka. The infection alone is bad enough, but I'd wager that arrow was laced with henbane poison. Let me guess—hallucinations, fever, barely conscious?"

Daka nodded. "Exactly that. Can you save him?"

"I'll do what I can," she said, pulling out a jar of dried Nerium leaves. "This paste is an antidote, but at this stage… I can't promise anything."

Daka stepped outside into the cool night air, his thoughts heavy. Near the well, he spotted Casius and Arla waiting silently, their expressions subdued. He approached the well, drawing up a bucket of water and tipping it over his head to clear his mind.

"You've brought these two for the favour, haven't you?" Marya's voice broke the quiet. She had appeared beside him, her gaze on the children.

"Yes," Daka admitted. "Not both—just the girl. She's an orphan we found near Niborya. Her family's gone, and she needs somewhere safe to stay. The boy is coming with me, but I can't take her into the army. She needs someone who can care for her."

Marya's face softened. Unbeknownst to Daka, she had longed for a child of her own, though she knew it was something she could never have.

"She can stay," Marya said finally. "I'll teach her to survive in a world full of men."

She walked over to Arla, placing an arm around her shoulders and guiding her toward the hut, speaking gently. Arla looked up at her, her fear replaced by curiosity.

Casius watched his sister go, his jaw set. He turned to Daka. "She'll be safe with her?"

"Marya's one of the strongest people I know, she might bark at us lot a bit but she's soft inside" Daka said. "Your sister will be fine."

Together, the two walked back to the camp, each carrying bundles of Popkin leaves to boil for the horses. The men looked at Daka in disbelief when he handed over the leaves; they'd presumed Marya was exaggerating to get them off her plants. They worked quickly to feed the antidote to the animals, who seemed grateful for the attention. As the others tended to their mounts, Daka sat by the fire, exhaustion finally claiming him. Within minutes, he was fast asleep.

Chapter 13

Spring 1308 Garhelm Forest

At first light, Daka and Casius bid farewell to Marya and Arla. The Prince's bodyguards were instructed to assist Marya if needed while staying out of her way. With little ceremony, the pair turned their horses back toward the camp to rejoin Grand Marshal Pesus and the rest of the army.

By the time they arrived, the camp was already alive with activity. Pesus had allowed an early stop the night before, ensuring the men were well-rested. Daka passed the perimeter guard and headed toward the Grand Marshal's tent, dismounting and handing his reins to Casius.

"Restock my saddlebag," Daka instructed, "and get her fed and watered. No doubt we'll be moving out soon."

The tent flap opened, and Pesus gestured for Daka to enter. Inside, the captains were gathered around a map laid across the central table, listening intently to Ghosht's report.

"There are at least five hundred of them," Ghosht began. "A second band arrived this morning, coming south from deeper within Garhelm Forest. Juntya is under their control—they've already opened the gates for the newcomers. The town is encircled by a wooden palisade. Open ground surrounds most of it, apart from the eastern side, which backs onto the forest. But moving an army through there quietly is nearly impossible."

Pesus stood in silence, processing the information. The tension was thick in the air. Bones broke it first, his gravelly voice cutting through the quiet.

"They have the advantage of the wall," he growled, "but they're cowards, holed up behind it. If we can draw some of them out, we'll slaughter them where they stand."

The mention of killing brought a grim smile to Bones's face, but Felix quickly intervened, his tone curt.

"And how exactly do you plan to draw five hundred men out from behind a perfectly good wall, Bones?"

Bones had no answer, his confidence faltering as he realised he hadn't thought that far ahead.

Daka stepped forward, speaking calmly. "We dangle a carrot so tempting that they can't resist. Bones, one of your men, Pax, was guarding Casius and his sister yesterday. He's about the Prince's height and bears a resemblance, rough around the edges though he may be. The enemy doesn't know the Prince isn't here with us. If we use Pax as a decoy—our 'carrot'—in a position that looks vulnerable, it might tempt them to send men out."

Pesus's eyes lit with understanding. "That's Pax, isn't it? And he carries one of the Prince's personal swords. Even under close inspection, it could work."

Bones grinned, eager to play his part. Without another word, he left the tent to fetch Pax.

Within the hour, the army was assembled and battle-ready. Ghoshte moved among the front rankers, selecting nine who could handle a bow. These men were outfitted with the captured bows and quivers of arrows, bringing the archery unit to thirty, including Casius. He was given light armour pulled from the supply carts and quickly fell in line with the others.

From the command tent emerged Pax, clad in the Prince's armour and helmet. A cavalryman followed him, carrying the royal banner—a visible signal of the Prince's supposed presence. Daka nodded approvingly as Pax mounted one of the spare horses and joined Felix and the cavalry, who disappeared into the woods to set up the ruse.

Pesus, Daka, Ghoshte, and Bones remained with the main force, giving Felix time to position his men. At midday, Pesus ordered the march. The army moved with disciplined efficiency, nerves buzzing quietly among the newer recruits.

As the column approached the southern edge of Juntya, the rhythmic march soothed Daka's thoughts. The soldiers, however, were tense. For many, this would be their first battle, and the risks were high. Their plan hinged on perfect execution. If Felix's squadron failed, the enemy would remain entrenched behind their walls.

The first soldiers stepped from the cover of the trees into the open ground. Immediately, a horn blared from the wooden palisade, alerting the enemy to their presence. Pesus halted the army just outside bow range, organising the men into formation. They had no intention of attacking the walls yet, not until darkness offered them the advantage.

Meanwhile, Pax and Casius rode with Felix's cavalry, weaving through the dense forest to circle around Juntya. The forest floor was treacherous, tangled with roots and strewn with obstacles. Their progress was painstakingly slow. Neither boy spoke much. Both were weighed down by the knowledge of their roles in the coming battle, each critical, each dangerous.

After an hour, Felix halted the group. The dense canopy

had blocked out much of the remaining daylight, making it hard to gauge their position. Felix sent two riders ahead to scout the forest's edge and determine their proximity to the walls.

When the scouts returned, they reported having overshot their target. Adjusting their course, Felix led the group toward the boggy patch Ghoshte had identified earlier. This was where Pax's ruse would play out.

Pax rode beside Felix, his youthful curiosity lighting up his face. "What was it like, serving in the army back then?" he asked, leaning slightly forward in his saddle. "Before all this. Were you always a captain?"

Felix's grip on the reins tightened ever so slightly, though his tone remained even. "No one starts as a captain, Pax. It was years of fighting on the frontiers, proving myself again and again. Back then, we didn't have the resources or the numbers we do now. Every battle felt like survival, not strategy."

Pax's eyes gleamed. "That sounds incredible. And Pesus? He's been in the army forever, hasn't he?"

Felix gave a short, dry laugh. "Yes. We were captains at the same time once. He had a knack for rallying men, I'll give him that." His jaw tensed momentarily, a shadow flickering across his expression. "Some people seem destined to rise, no matter what."

Pax missed the undercurrent in Felix's tone, his excitement bubbling over. "So, you've both been serving for the same length of time? That's amazing. I can't imagine leading alongside someone like him."

Felix's smile was tight as he glanced ahead to where the trail wound deeper into the forest. "Yes," he said lightly, the bitterness in his voice barely detectable. "Amazing." Without another word, he nudged his horse forward, the moment passing as quickly as it had come.

By the time they reached the edge of the forest, night was falling. Torches flickered along Juntya's walls, and orders echoed faintly from within. The enemy likely felt secure behind their defences.

Felix turned to Pax with a smirk. "Well, my Prince," he said, his tone dripping with mock formality, "time to shine."

Pax adjusted his helmet, tightened his chin strap, and exchanged a nod with his flag bearer.

Chapter 14

Spring 1308 Garhelm Forest
Marya's Hut

The small hut was warm, its atmosphere steeped in a faint, soothing scent of herbs and simmering broth. A soft fire crackled in the hearth, casting flickering shadows that danced on the wooden walls, lending the space an air of tranquillity. Outside, the forest murmured gently, the rustling of leaves and occasional birdsong creating a calming backdrop. Yet inside, the world was hushed and still, except for the occasional laboured breaths of Althern, who lay motionless on the cot.

He had been hovering between consciousness and fevered delirium for days. At times, his body burned with heat, leaving him thrashing weakly against the confines of his illness. At others, he was unnervingly calm, his breaths shallow and fragile. Marya, ever vigilant, had remained by his side throughout it all. Her hands moved with practised precision as she crushed herbs, checked bandages, and brewed teas, her movements a testament to her skill and resilience.

Arla watched from a corner of the room, perched on a small stool. Her wide eyes missed nothing, following every motion as Marya worked. Though she didn't speak much, her curiosity was evident in the way she leaned forward, absorbing every detail.

"Arla," Marya said without looking up, her voice calm yet commanding, "fetch me the jar of feverroot paste from the shelf."

The girl immediately sprang to her feet, eager to be useful. She returned moments later, clutching a small, weathered jar in her hands.

"Good girl," Marya said with a faint smile, taking the jar. "Now, watch closely. See how I spread it over the wound? Just enough to cover it, not too thick, or it won't let the skin breathe."

Arla leaned in, her small frame almost trembling with focus as she observed the careful application of the paste. The wound on Althern's back and side was healing, though the progress was painstakingly slow. Angry red edges framed the gash, a stubborn reminder of the arrow that had pierced him, but Marya's treatments seemed to soothe it.

A faint murmur broke the silence. "Water," Althern croaked, his voice barely more than a whisper, hoarse from days of fever.

Marya immediately set the jar aside and reached for the wooden cup on the table nearby. "Easy now," she murmured, slipping her arm under his shoulders and carefully lifting him upright.

Althern groaned softly as the movement aggravated his wound, but he accepted the cup eagerly, drinking deeply. The cool water soothed his parched throat, and he sagged back against the pillows with a faint sigh when he'd finished.

"Thank you," he managed, his voice weak but clear.

"You're welcome," Marya replied, her tone gentle yet firm.

For a moment, their eyes met. Despite the shadows of fatigue etched into his face, Althern mustered a faint, grateful smile.

"You're a good healer," he said, his voice tinged with genuine admiration.

Marya chuckled softly, shaking her head. "And you're a terrible patient."

Althern's smile widened faintly, though it was interrupted by a wince as he adjusted his position. "I suppose I deserve that," he said, his tone edged with self-deprecating humour.

From her place by the fire, Arla tilted her head, watching the exchange with an expression that suggested she was trying to decipher something unspoken between the two adults.

As the days stretched on, Althern's strength began to return, though his recovery was far from complete. The fever clung to him stubbornly, its grip loosening only inch by inch. Through it all, Marya remained a steadfast presence, tending to him with care that was both efficient and kind.

She often spoke to him in soft, measured tones as she worked, telling stories about the forest, the people who had once lived there, and the properties of the plants she used. At first, Althern listened in silence, too weak to respond. But as his strength slowly returned, he began to join in, asking questions or offering dry, sardonic remarks that sometimes coaxed a laugh from Marya.

"I don't know how you do it," Althern said one evening, his voice stronger than it had been in days.

"Do what?" Marya asked, glancing up from the poultice she was preparing.

"Keep everything so... calm," he replied, gesturing vaguely to the cosy interior of the hut. "You live out here in the middle of nowhere, patching up fools like me, and you make it look effortless."

Marya smiled, though there was a flicker of something unreadable in her eyes. "It's not effortless," she said simply. "But it's what I know. And sometimes, it's enough."

Althern studied her, his brow furrowed. "You're stronger than most of the men I've fought beside," he said, his tone almost reverent.

Marya let out a soft laugh, a spark of humour brightening her expression. "I imagine that's not a particularly high bar to clear."

For the first time in days, Althern laughed, a quiet, wheezing sound that ended in a cough but left him smiling nonetheless.

Arla, meanwhile, absorbed everything she could. She watched Marya closely, her sharp eyes following the healer's every movement as she brewed teas and prepared salves. The girl asked countless questions, her curiosity insatiable.

"Why feverroot?" Arla asked one afternoon, watching as Marya crushed dried leaves into powder.

"Because it cools the body and fights fever from within," Marya explained. "But it's potent, so you have to be careful with the amount you use."

Arla nodded solemnly, committing the information to memory. Later, as Marya prepared dinner, Arla sat by Althern's side, her small hands folded neatly in her lap.

"Are you going to be king?" she asked suddenly, breaking the comfortable silence.

Althern turned his head to look at her, his expression thoughtful. "That's the plan," he said after a pause.

"Do you want to be?"

The question seemed to catch him off guard. He frowned slightly, his gaze drifting toward the ceiling. "Sometimes what we want doesn't matter," he said eventually. "Sometimes it's about what needs to be done."

Arla considered this, her brow furrowed in concentration. "I think you'll be a good king," she said with quiet conviction.

Althern's lips curved into a faint smile, and his voice softened. "Thank you, Arla."

That evening, after Althern had fallen into a restless sleep, Marya and Arla sat by the fire. Marya's hands were busy mending a tear in one of the prince's shirts, while Arla idly poked at the flames with a stick.

"Do you think he'll be all right?" Arla asked, her voice small.

Marya nodded, her gaze steady. "He's strong. And stubborn. He'll pull through."

Arla was quiet for a moment, then glanced up at Marya. "He likes you," she said matter-of-factly.

Marya blinked, startled. "What?"

"He likes you," Arla repeated, her tone certain. "I can tell."

Marya laughed softly, shaking her head. "You have an overactive imagination, Arla."

But as she returned to her mending, her eyes flicked briefly toward the sleeping prince. For just a moment, her expression softened, but whether it was sadness, hope, or something else entirely, even she couldn't quite tell.

Chapter 15

Spring 1308 Juntya Village

The moonlight seeped through the thick canopy of trees, casting a pale silver glow over the forest. Pax sat rigid atop his borrowed horse, his grip on the reins so tight that his knuckles had turned white. The royal insignia of the prince fluttered faintly beside him, held high by the flag bearer, who rode silently at his side. Twenty cavalrymen flanked them, their faces shadowed in the dim light, their armour faintly glinting as they prepared for their high-stakes deception.

"Remember," Captain Felix had told him earlier, his tone calm but unyielding, "Your job isn't to fight. You're to sell the illusion. Look convincing, hold their attention, and then play your part. The rest of us will handle the killing."

The weight of those words hung heavy in Pax's chest as the group emerged from the treeline. Before them stretched a vast expanse of open ground—around seven hundred paces of exposed terrain leading directly to Juntya's wooden walls. No cover, no chance to hide. Just the cold night air, the pounding of hooves, and the weight of the role he had to play.

The boy cut a striking figure as he rode toward the walls,

the royal banner fluttering behind him. The enemy shouted from the battlements, their confusion palpable. Within moments, torches flared brighter as they scrambled to react.

From the treeline, Felix and the cavalry watched silently. Casius, his bow resting in his lap, tightened his grip on the reins. The plan was in motion. All that remained was to see whether the enemy would take the bait.

Above the palisade, faint torchlight flickered, barely illuminating the enemy archers perched atop the wall. As the cavalry charged forward, the enemy loosed their first volley of arrows. The shafts hissed through the air, landing well short of their mark. The distance was still too great, and for now, the riders remained untouched.

Pax's thoughts drifted, unbidden, to his parents. He imagined them hiding somewhere nearby in the forest, waiting for rescue. Perhaps they had escaped. Perhaps they were still alive. But deep down, he knew the truth. If they had stayed in Juntya, they were most likely dead. And if they had fled, they would have done so long before now. He forced the thought from his mind, swallowing the lump in his throat. There would be time to grieve later. If he survived.

The bog came into view, its dark surface glinting faintly in the moonlight. The air grew heavy with the stench of stagnant water. Felix's instructions rang clear in his mind: Make it look real.

Pax yanked the reins sharply, forcing his horse to rear. With all the dramatic flair he could muster, he flung himself from the saddle, landing in the marsh with a resounding splash. Pain shot through his shoulder as it collided with the ground, a sickening crunch confirming that something had gone wrong. Gasping for air, he lay sprawled in the mud, struggling to right himself.

Around him, the other cavalrymen played their parts,

tumbling from their mounts into the muck with practised chaos. Horses scattered, whinnying in feigned panic, adding to the illusion of a charge gone disastrously wrong. The flag bearer blew the retreat signal, a long, mournful note that echoed across the battlefield and reached the treeline where the rest of the army waited.

Grand Marshal Pesus stood watching from the edge of the forest, his sharp gaze tracking Pax as the boy hit the ground. The fall had been alarmingly convincing, perhaps too convincing.

"Gods," Pesus muttered, narrowing his eyes. "That boy might've actually broken something."

But there was no time to dwell on it. The plan was unfolding, and so far, it was working.

"Advance!" Pesus barked, his voice cutting through the air like a whip.

Daka's knights surged forward, their shields raised high in an impenetrable wall. Behind them, Ghosht's archers followed, each man concealed by the towering shields of the knights. The front rankers spread out into a wide but shallow formation, creating the illusion of a larger force pressing forward across the open ground.

The rhythmic pounding of boots echoed ominously as the knights closed the distance to Juntya. Above the gate, the enemy archers adjusted their aim, raining arrows down onto the advancing force. The sound of projectiles clattering against shields filled the air, and here and there, knights fell, arrows finding gaps in their armour.

"Hold steady!" Daka's commanding voice roared. "Shields high! Eyes on me!"

The knights slowed their march, bracing themselves under the relentless hail of arrows. Their arms trembled with the effort of holding their shields aloft, but they pressed on.

Pesus scanned the palisade above the gates, searching for any sign of hesitation among the enemy. He didn't have to wait long.

A deep horn blast cut through the night air, and the heavy wooden gates creaked open. A column of enemy soldiers streamed out, their weapons glinting in the faint light. For a moment, it seemed as though they would charge directly at Daka's line. Pesus held his breath.

At the last moment, the enemy veered left, wheeling towards the bog where Pax and the cavalrymen lay. Pesus allowed himself a small smile. "Hook's in."

The enemy soldiers waded into the marsh, their boots sinking into the thick mud. Water and filth clung to their legs, slowing their movements to a crawl. Above, Ghoshte's archers lit their fire arrows, the flames casting an eerie glow over the battlefield.

"First volley—loose!" Ghosht ordered.

The flaming arrows arced through the sky, their fiery tips slamming into the gates of Juntya. Sparks scattered across the wood, some catching hold. The enemy reacted instantly, slamming the gates shut to protect their stronghold.

"Second volley, higher arc!" Ghosht called.

The next wave of arrows struck the palisade above the gates. Flames roared to life, licking hungrily at the dry timber. Enemy archers scrambled for safety, their positions consumed by the fire.

In the bog, Pax forced himself to his feet, his sword trembling in his hands as the enemy soldiers closed in. His heart thundered in his chest, the weight of his role pressing down on him.

"NOW!" he shouted, his voice cracking with desperation.

The cavalrymen sprang to life, leaping from the mud with

weapons drawn. Mud and water splattered in every direction as blades clashed. The shallow bog erupted into chaos.

Pax's first opponent staggered towards him, exhaustion evident in the man's movements. Pax lunged, his blade sinking deep into the soldier's chest. Another enemy rushed him with a hunting knife, slashing wildly. Pax felt a hot, wet sensation in his thigh as the blade found its mark, but he gritted his teeth, finishing the man with a swift thrust.

The ground trembled as Felix and his cavalry smashed into the rear of the enemy column. Having hooked round the northern flank of the enemy from the cover of the forest. Horses thundered through the bog, trampling soldiers underfoot. Swords flashed, cutting down men with brutal efficiency. The charge sent waves of panic through the enemy ranks, their formation collapsing in chaos.

"Pull back! Re-form the line!" Felix shouted, his voice rising over the din. His riders regrouped, preparing for another devastating charge.

Behind the enemy, Bones and his front rankers arrived in a bloodthirsty charge, cutting off any hope of retreat. Bones led the assault, his oversized sword cleaving through armour and flesh with terrifying ease. His men moved with ruthless precision, their shields forming an unbreakable wall as they advanced.

The battle descended into brutal close combat. The bog became a killing field, the water churning with blood and bodies. The enemy, trapped between the cavalry, the knights, and Ghoshte's relentless archers, fell rapidly.

Bones planted his boot on a fallen soldier, yanking his blade free with a grunt. Around him, his men advanced steadily, cutting down the remaining enemy soldiers. The battlefield was a cacophony of screams, clashing weapons, and the sickening thud of bodies hitting the ground. Bones stood at the centre of the chaos, his massive blade already slick with blood as he swung it in wide, devastating arcs. Around him, his men fought valiantly, but they were being picked off.The cries of the dying filled the night, mingling with the crackle of flames from the burning palisade.He saw one of his front rankers, a young soldier barely old enough to grow a beard, fall to his knees, clutching a fatal wound as an enemy blade pierced his chest. Bones's vision blurred with rage, his breaths coming in ragged, animalistic snarls. He surged forward like a storm unleashed, his strikes becoming heavier, faster, each blow aimed to utterly destroy. The enemy scattered before him, but it wasn't enough. The sight of his comrades dying fuelled a fire in his chest, turning his anger into a relentless force. "Come on, then!" he roared, his voice a thunderous challenge above the din. "Let's see how long you can last!"

When the last of the enemy fell, silence descended. Bones turned to his men, his voice carrying over the smouldering wreckage.

"Form up! Face the village! At the march!"

From his position, Pesus surveyed the burning gates of Juntya. The plan had worked, but a gnawing sense of unease crept into his thoughts. The victory had come too easily.

"This isn't over," he muttered, his eyes narrowing. "Not by a long shot."

Chapter 16

Spring 1308 Juntya Village

Bones' crew brought forward tools from the mule carts, hammering hooks into the charred remains of Juntya's village gates. Blackened and brittle from the fire, the gate didn't hold for long. With a thunderous crash, the structure gave way as the front rankers tugged the ropes, sending a cloud of ash and sparks spiralling into the night sky. The men shielded their faces as soot rained down, leaving them streaked with black. The fiery glow of the smouldering timber illuminated their grim expressions.

"Move aside! Let the knights through!" bellowed Bones, his voice cutting through the commotion. His men scrambled into two lines, clearing the path for Daka's heavily armoured knights to advance.

Jogging at the heart of his formation, Daka kept his shield raised, the polished steel of his armour gleaming faintly in the firelight. The knights marched with precision, their shields forming an impenetrable wall. Beyond the burning gateway, Juntya stretched out in darkness, its narrow streets eerily quiet. Torches flickered here and there, casting jagged shadows across the broken village.

"Eyes on the alleys," Daka called, his voice low but steady. "Anything could be hiding in there."

The knights pushed forward, their boots thudding heavily on the cobblestones. The silence of the village was unnerving. Apart from the crackling of flames and the distant creak of windblown wood, there was nothing. No movement. No sound. Only the occasional corpse lying sprawled in the dirt hinted at the chaos that had unfolded earlier. The absence of resistance set Daka's nerves on edge.

The main pathway led directly to the trader's square in the centre of the village. In better times, this space would have been bustling with merchants and travellers. Now, it was shrouded in darkness, its emptiness oppressive. Daka glanced to his left, searching the palisade for any sign of Ghoshte and his archers, who were supposed to be shadowing his movements. The shadows made it impossible to spot them, but Daka trusted they were there, watching from above. Still, unease prickled at the edges of his mind.

Then it came—a piercing scream. High-pitched and raw, it echoed through the village, cutting through the oppressive stillness like a blade. Daka's heart lurched, the sound sending a shiver down his spine. The scream had come from the far side of the village, near the wall. He caught a flicker of movement—Ghoshte sprinting along the palisade towards the source of the noise. The captain's voice soon followed, sharp and urgent.

"Daka! Get your men to the wall—NOW!"

Without hesitation, Daka raised his sword. "Knights, on me! Move!"

The formation shifted, and the knights broke into a jog, their heavy boots pounding against the dirt as they followed him through the narrow streets. The wall was only a hundred paces away, and they reached it quickly. There, Ghoshte stood on the parapet, staring out into the dark expanse beyond Juntya. Beneath him was a gaping hole in the wooden barricade, a chaotic mess of splintered beams and debris large enough for several men to pass through side by side.

"Shields up!" Daka ordered, his knights forming a defensive line in front of the breach. They raised their shields, creating an impenetrable barrier against whatever threat might emerge.

"What happened?" Daka demanded, turning to Ghoshte. The captain's face was pale, his expression grim.

"They've made a breach," Ghoshte said, nodding to the gap in the wall. "As we came through the gate they were fleeing into the forest at the back" Ghosthe shook his head "Felix and the boy, they were dragged from their horses. The cavalry didn't stand a chance. The enemy swarmed them."

Daka felt the blood drain from his face. The faux prince,Pax,had been part of the cavalry sent to intercept the enemy's retreat. If Felix and his riders had been overwhelmed, it was unlikely Pax had escaped. The plan had worked, but at a greater cost than any of them had anticipated.

He turned sharply to one of his men. "Go. Find Pesus. Tell him what's happened."

The soldier saluted and took off at a sprint, vanishing into the shadows. Daka's knights held their line, their breaths heavy in the still night air. Beyond the wall, the cries of the dying drifted toward them—desperate, guttural sounds that sent a chill through even the most seasoned soldiers. Some voices pleaded for help, others faded into weak, shuddering sobs. The noise clawed at Daka's resolve.

Moments later, Pesus arrived, his horse's hooves clattering on the cobblestones. He reined in sharply near the breach, his eyes scanning the battlefield beyond. "Report," he snapped.

Ghoshte stepped forward. "The cavalry was surrounded. Felix is down, and the boy was taken. I saw them being dragged from their horses before the enemy disappeared into the treeline."

Pesus swore under his breath, his jaw tightening. He turned in his saddle, his sharp gaze tracing the outline of the wall. Finally, he spoke. "They must have ridden to cut the enemy off. We hold the village tonight. Fortify the walls, repair the breach, and bar the gates. No one leaves until dawn. At first light, we search the battlefield for survivors."

Daka hesitated. "Marshal, the men out there, some of them are still alive. Could we not send a small party to put them out of their misery?"

Pesus's eyes snapped to him, blazing with frustration. "And risk losing more men to an ambush? No. Those are my orders, Captain."

The words stung, but Daka said nothing. He understood the logic, even if it made his stomach churn.

Bones' engineers worked tirelessly through the night, using beams scavenged from burnt-out houses to patch the breach in the wall. The villagers had fled long before the bandits' arrival, leaving behind only abandoned homes and the faint scent of smoke.

As the adrenaline of battle faded, exhaustion set in. Daka dismissed his knights to rest, but he found no comfort in the stillness of the night. The cries from beyond the walls echoed in his mind, their haunting cadence a cruel reminder of the day's losses. Unable to sit idly by, he climbed the parapet to find Ghoshte.

The archer captain stood with two of his men, both

holding nocked arrows tipped with fire. "Who's still out there?" Daka asked quietly.

"One of the cavalry," Ghoshte replied. He gestured to the archer, who loosed his flaming arrow into the darkness. For a brief moment, the scene was illuminated—a soldier lay trapped beneath his fallen horse, his lower body crushed beyond repair.

"He won't last the night," Ghoshte muttered. "Finish it."

The second archer took aim, his arrow cutting through the night with a faint whistle. The soldier's cries ceased abruptly, the silence that followed heavy and suffocating. Daka stared out at the fading light of the fire arrows, a knot forming in his stomach.

A runner arrived soon after, summoning him and Ghoshte to the command tent.

Inside, Pesus stood by the brazier, his face shadowed by flickering light. "None of the cavalry returned," he said grimly. "Felix and Pax are gone. Fifty men lost. Ghoshte, you held without losses. Bones, your men fared the worst."

Bones grunted, his face hard as stone.

Pesus continued, his voice laced with fatigue. "Forty seven dead. Twenty nine wounded. If the enemy believes they have the prince, they'll likely use him as a bargaining chip. I'll send word to the king at first light. We'll give the warband a head start, then move to block their retreat."

Ghoshte frowned. "That's a dangerous gamble, Marshal."

Pesus nodded. "It is. But it's the only move we have." He straightened, his expression resolute. "Rest while you can. The day after tomorrow, we march."

The captains exchanged weary glances before leaving the tent. As Daka walked through the camp, the cries of the dying faded into memory, but the weight of the losses remained heavy on his shoulders. The battle for Juntya had been won, but the cost was far greater than anyone had expected.

Chapter 17

Spring 1308 Deep into Garhelm forest

Faintly aware of something nudging his side, Pax grumbled and rolled over. A second later, a sharp sting struck his temple as a small rock bounced off his head, jolting him upright. Blinking groggily, he spotted Captain Felix sitting across from him, his hands bound but a grin tugging at his lips.

"I reckon you could sleep through a bloody cavalry charge," Felix whispered, his voice low but laced with dry humour.

Pax groaned, rubbing the spot where the rock had hit, before glancing around. They were confined in a crude wooden cage mounted on a cart, parked deep within the enemy's camp. The smell of damp earth and unwashed bodies was thick in the air. Fifteen paces away, six bandits lounged by a fire, passing around a wineskin and arguing in slurred tones. The camp stretched into the shadows beyond, disorderly and grim. There were no tents, no wagons of supplies—just men sprawled on the ground or leaning against tree trunks, their movements slow and weary.

The reality of their situation crashed down on Pax as he flexed his bound wrists. The coarse rope had rubbed his skin raw, and he winced at the sharp sting. His hands felt numb from the cold, and he struggled to work some feeling back into his fingers.

Felix shuffled closer to him, his voice dropping to a whisper. "They've been in twice since you were out. Still think you're the Prince."

Pax frowned, shaking his head as if to clear it. "I'm not, though. They'll figure it out soon enough."

Felix raised an eyebrow. "Will they? These aren't city men, Pax. They're Garhelm forest folk—they've probably never laid eyes on the Prince, or the King for that matter. If they think you're Althern, they'll keep you alive." He paused, a flicker of grim amusement crossing his face. "Better odds than telling them the truth, I'd wager."

The boy didn't respond, his brow furrowing as he absorbed Felix's words. They sat in uneasy silence, their ears tuned to the crackle of the distant fire and the guttural laughter of the bandits. Felix had remained awake through the jolting cart ride that had brought them deeper into the woods, his instincts refusing to let him rest. Pax, though, had drifted in and out of a restless sleep. Now, surrounded by the enemy, the reality of their predicament weighed heavily on him.

As the first light of dawn filtered through the forest canopy, their jailer approached—a hulking brute of a man with a jagged scar running the length of his cheek. He carried himself with a sluggish confidence, unlocking the cage with a rusty key before motioning for them to step out.

Stiff from the cold, Pax stumbled to his feet, his muscles protesting with every move. He followed the jailer, his stomach twisting as the smell of roasting rabbit from nearby fires made his hunger gnaw painfully. Felix walked beside him, his face impassive despite the ropes biting into his wrists.

At the far end of the camp, they came to a clearing where a grim-looking man sat perched on a tree stump. His dark hair was streaked with grey, and a deep scar bisected his left cheek. A suit of gleaming, light armour lay beside him on the ground, out of place amidst the ragged surroundings. Draped over the tree trump next to him was a long rough looking coat. His left arm hung limp, blood soaking through the woollen shirt at his armpit, but his eyes were sharp and assessing.

The man's gaze locked on Pax, his lips curling into a cold, mocking smile. "You're younger than I imagined, Althern. For a boy who's supposedly won victories worthy of song, you seem... underwhelming."

Pax froze, realising the man believed him to be the Prince. Felix gave him a sharp look, a silent order to play along.

"I... I had good captains to guide me," Pax stammered, his voice shaky.

The man's smile deepened, though it didn't reach his eyes. "A diplomat already. How precious." He leaned forward, his piercing gaze boring into Pax's. "Let's hope your charm is enough to make your father see reason. My employer wants what's rightfully his. Perhaps a bit ahead of schedule, but who's counting?"

Felix seized the opportunity to speak. "Prince Rok? You work for the Brotherhood?"

The man's smile shifted into something darker, his amusement sharp and dangerous. "Rok? No. I don't kneel for boys playing at kings. I take their gold, serve their purposes, but I belong to no one."

He gestured to his bloodied arm, his tone almost casual.

"My name is Widow. Remember it well. I've left more widows and orphans than your so-called Prince has followers. My allegiance is to opportunity, not thrones."

His calculating gaze slid to Felix. "And you? Not some lowly foot soldier, judging by that armour."

"Felix. Captain of Cavalry," the soldier replied, straightening his back despite the ropes binding his wrists.

Widow rose slowly, wincing as he adjusted his injured arm. He radiated an air of quiet menace, his movements deliberate. "A prince and a captain. King Apius should be grateful I've spared his toys. He will pay dearly for their return." His tone dripped with mockery. "Of course, I'll make sure he understands your safety hinges on how... agreeable he is."

Pax opened his mouth to retort, but Felix nudged him subtly, warning him to hold his tongue. Widow caught the movement and chuckled, a low, menacing sound.

"Ah, the captain thinks himself clever. Careful, Felix. My patience for insolence is thinner than this shirt." Widow gestured to a nearby guard. "Return them to their cage. Feed them well. I want them alive when I start sending pieces to the King."

He turned to leave but paused, looking over his shoulder. "Oh, and Captain, you must train your archers better. One of them got a lucky shot. Next time, I'll return the favour." He touched the bloodstained fabric covering his arm and smirked coldly. "I never miss twice."

The guards hauled Pax and Felix back to the cage, where two bowls of rabbit stew awaited them. They ate in silence, the warm food doing little to lift their spirits. Pax's appetite waned quickly, the weight of Widow's words pressing heavily on him.

Felix leaned closer, his voice low. "That's no forest brute. He's a wolf in armour. We're in trouble."

Pax nodded, swallowing hard. Widow's cold, intelligent malice lingered in his thoughts, leaving his skin crawling and his stomach churning.

Chapter 18

Spring 1308 Garhelm Forest
Marya's hut

The dull ache in Althern's shoulder was a constant reminder of the wound, but it had healed well. Standing at the well, he steeled himself to splash the cool water over his skin. The sun was just rising, its golden rays turning the steaming ground into a hazy mirage. He shivered as he plunged his hands into the water.

Around the corner of her workshop, Marya appeared, her stride purposeful, a basket in her arms. Without breaking pace, she marched up to him and thrust it against his chest, the suddenness catching him off guard.

"Here. Make yourself useful," she said, flashing him a brief, mischievous smile before meeting his eyes for the briefest of moments. "Take those inside and start crushing your medicine. You've seen me do it enough times by now."

Before he could reply, she spun on her heel and strode off, Arla trailing behind her like a shadow. Althern watched them leave, his gaze lingering on the healer's retreating figure. Her dark hair bounced with every step, catching the light. There was something about her that pulled his attention effortlessly—her unbothered defiance, her striking beauty, the way she moved as if nothing and no one could ever shake her.

Shaking his head, he forced himself to focus, plunging his hands back into the water and splashing his face to snap out of his thoughts. After finishing, he grabbed the basket and headed into the small hut where he had been staying. Inside, the air was cold, the embers from the previous night's fire barely alive. He added thin kindling to coax the flames back to life before turning his attention to the task Marya had given him.

The plants in the basket needed grinding into a thick, bitter paste, his daily medicine to purge the poison still lingering in his blood from the bandit's arrow. The concoction was foul-tasting and smelled even worse, but he didn't dare skip a dose. If there was one thing he'd learned quickly, it was that Marya's word was not to be taken lightly.

The door creaked open behind him, letting in a sliver of cold morning air. Marya stepped inside, placing a pair of gloves on the table. She leaned casually against the back of a chair, her eyes fixed on him with an intensity that made him pause.

"Where's Arla?" Althern asked, breaking the silence.

"She's practising with her bow," Marya replied without looking away. "With your men."

Her lips curved slightly, but the smile didn't reach her eyes. She let out a sigh. "You know," she began, her tone casual but carrying an edge, "if you're going to stare at me while I'm walking away, it's best not to do it when Arla can see you."

Althern froze, his heart suddenly racing. "Stare?" he stammered, his voice rising in pitch. "I'm not sure what you mean."

Marya raised an eyebrow and stepped forward, closing

the distance between them. "Oh, I think you do," she said, her voice quiet but charged with meaning.

Althern tried to step back, but his movement was stopped by the workbench pressing into his lower back. Marya took another step, the space between them disappearing until he could feel the faint brush of her body against his. She reached out, taking his hands and placing them lightly on her hips.

His breath caught as her touch sent a jolt through him. He froze, unsure whether to pull away or remain rooted where he stood. Her scent surrounded him—herbs mixed with something earthy and warm—and his thoughts became a tangled mess of emotions.

"I... Marya, I didn't mean—"

"Don't," she interrupted, her sharp gaze cutting through his words. "There's no need for words, Althern. I know exactly what you mean." Her tone softened slightly, but it didn't lose its weight. "Do you think I don't notice the way you look at me when you think I'm not paying attention?"

He flushed, his face heating as she held his hands in place. "I wasn't staring," he mumbled weakly, trying to pull his hands away, but her grip tightened—not painfully, but enough to make her point.

"Thinking, then?" she said, tilting her head, a faint smirk tugging at the corner of her lips. "Well, if you were, it's clear you weren't thinking straight."

Althern swallowed hard, the intensity of her presence making it nearly impossible to form a coherent thought. His mind raced, his responsibilities, his position, the expectations that constantly weighed on him. All seemed to vanish in her presence.

Marya's expression shifted, her teasing replaced by something deeper. "You know," she said, her voice quieter now, "I've met men like you before. Men who hide behind titles, who bury what they want beneath duty and responsibility. But let me be clear. I'm not some conquest or a passing indulgence."

Her words struck him like a blow. He straightened, her meaning cutting through the haze in his mind. "That's not what this is," he said quickly, his voice firm, though there was an edge of desperation to it. "I'm not like that."

Marya studied him for a moment, her sharp gaze softening slightly. "Then prove it," she said simply. She stepped back, releasing his hands, but her eyes stayed locked on his. "Stop hiding behind your crown and your royal blood. Show me who you are, Althern. Show me the man behind the prince."

Her challenge hung in the air, the weight of it settling heavily in his chest. He looked away, his voice dropping. "I don't know how to be anything else," he admitted.

Marya smiled then, her expression tinged with a rare tenderness. She reached out, brushing a hand lightly against his arm before stepping away. "Then learn," she said, her voice steady but not unkind. "Learn before it's too late. You're more than a title, Althern. But if you don't figure that out, you'll lose more than just yourself."

Without another word, she turned and walked out, leaving Althern standing by the workbench, his thoughts in turmoil.

As the door creaked shut behind her, he let out a shaky breath. For the first time in years, something other than the weight of the crown stirred within him. It wasn't duty or responsibility, it was something raw, something real, something he wasn't sure he understood and for once, he wanted to understand.

Chapter 19

Spring 1308 Juntya Village

The pale morning light filtered through the forest canopy, casting shifting patterns of green and gold on the forest floor. The camp near Juntya was stirring, soldiers preparing for the day with the occasional bark of orders cutting through the calm. Casius was already awake, seated on the edge of the campfire. His cot sat empty behind him as he ran his whetstone along the edge of his father's hunting knife. The rhythmic scrape of steel on stone filled the air as he focused on honing the blade to perfection. His stomach growled, but he ignored it, determined to finish his task.

"Not bad work for a boy," came a gruff voice from behind him.

Casius glanced up to see Ghoshte, the wiry captain of the archers, standing over him. The man's bow was slung across his back, and a brace of freshly killed rabbits dangled from his belt. His angular face was smeared with dirt, and his sharp, piercing eyes seemed to miss nothing.

"You're coming with me today," Ghoshte said without preamble, his tone more command than suggestion. "I'll teach you to hunt properly. The army needs food, and you need to learn."

Casius bristled, setting his knife down as he met Ghoshte's gaze. "I already know how to hunt," he said, his voice tinged with defiance.

Ghoshte smirked, amused by the boy's boldness. "Oh, you can bring down a boar, can you? Impressive. But hunting isn't just about prey, boy. The forest is a battlefield. Let's see what you really know."

Without waiting for a response, Ghoshte turned and strode into the trees, his movements fluid and confident. For a moment, Casius hesitated, glancing at the knife in his hand before sheathing it. Grabbing his bow, he hurried after the captain, his curiosity outweighing his irritation.

They moved deeper into the forest, the towering trees closing around them. Ghoshte moved with an ease that suggested years of practice, pointing out subtle details that Casius would have missed. He crouched by a broken branch, brushing his fingers against faint hoofprints in the mud.

"Deer," Ghoshte said, his voice low but clear. "Passed through last night."

Casius nodded, committing the details to memory. "And if it were people?" he asked, his voice quieter now.

Ghoshte turned his sharp gaze on the boy, his expression unreadable. "Then you'd look for different signs, bootprints instead of hooves, snapped twigs higher up, bits of fabric on branches. Even the remains of a fire, if they were sloppy." He straightened, brushing dirt from his hands. "The principles are the same, though. Find the trail, read the signs, and follow them."

They continued in silence for a time, the crunch of leaves underfoot mingling with the distant calls of birds. Suddenly,

Ghoshte froze, raising a hand to halt Casius. He crouched low, his eyes fixed on a patch of foliage up ahead.

"There," he murmured, nodding toward a hare nibbling at some leaves a short distance from them. "Your shot. Slow draw. Aim for the heart."

Casius nocked an arrow, drawing the string back steadily. His arms stayed firm, despite the tension thrumming through his body. Taking a deep breath, he exhaled slowly and released. The arrow flew true, striking the hare cleanly and dropping it where it stood.

"Good," Ghoshte said with a nod of approval. "You've got a good aim. That'll serve you well. So long as you can control your breathing"

Casius retrieved the hare, his chest swelling slightly with pride. But his thoughts lingered on something else. "Have you ever hunted people?" he asked, his voice barely above a whisper.

Ghoshte didn't answer immediately. He crouched by the hare, inspecting the kill with a practised eye. Finally, he spoke, his voice quieter than before. "Yes. And it's not something you do lightly. Hunting men is different. They think. They adapt. And they remember."

The weight of his words pressed on Casius, but he said nothing. As they roasted the hare over a small fire, Ghoshte leaned back against a fallen log, staring into the flames.

"You think hunting's just about food," Ghoshte said, his tone thoughtful. "But it's more than that. It's about understanding the land, reading the patterns, knowing the prey. That's what keeps you alive out here."

Casius nodded, though his thoughts lingered on Ghoshte's earlier admission. After a moment, he asked quietly, "When you hunted people... were they bad men?"

Ghoshte's sharp eyes met his, their intensity almost overwhelming. "Bad? Good? Those words mean nothing in the forest. What mattered was that they wanted me dead, and I wasn't ready to die."

The boy fell silent, his hands tightening around his bow. Ghoshte softened slightly, his tone losing some of its edge. "You've got potential, Casius. But if you let anger or vengeance guide you, you'll make mistakes. And mistakes in the forest will kill you."

The faint stench of decay hit Casius' nose, pulling him from his thoughts. He froze, his body tensing instinctively. Ghoshte noticed immediately, raising a hand to calm the boy.

"Stay close," he murmured, his voice low as he moved toward the source of the smell.

They emerged into a small clearing, where a broken cart lay surrounded by the bodies of villagers from Juntya. The sight hit Casius like a blow, his stomach turning as his gaze fell on the lifeless figures.

Ghoshte crouched by one of the bodies, a man whose throat had been slashed. "Didn't make it far," he said grimly. "Caught while fleeing. Forest men, most likely, a small group."

Casius' eyes landed on a young boy slumped against a tree, his lifeless gaze fixed on the canopy above. In his hand, he clutched a tattered doll. He dropped to his knees beside him, his throat tightening painfully.

"He's just a kid," he choked out, reaching out to gently close his eyes. The image of Arla flashed in his mind, twisting the knife in his heart.

Ghoshte watched in silence, his expression hard but not unkind. "This is what the forest men leave behind," he said softly. "You needed to see this."

Casius clenched his fists, tears stinging his eyes. "Why? Why him? Why any of them?"

"They were in the way," Ghoshte said simply. "And that's reason enough for men like these."

The boy's anger flared, burning hot in his chest, but it was tempered by a deep, aching sadness. His gaze lingered on the doll before he looked up at Ghoshte. "We can't leave them like this."

Ghoshte nodded, his expression sombre. "We'll bury them. It's the least we can do."

They worked in silence, digging shallow graves with their hands and whatever tools they could find. When they finished, Casius lingered by the boys's grave, pressing the doll into the earth before stepping back.

As they made their way back to camp, Ghoshte glanced at the boy. "You'll remember this moment, Casius. The forest teaches harsh lessons. Don't forget it."

"I won't," Casius said, his voice steady despite the weight in his chest.

By the time they returned to camp, the sun was dipping below the horizon. Soldiers huddled around fires, passing bowls of stew and speaking in hushed tones. Casius dropped the hare near the cooking pit and sat by a fire, staring into the flickering flames.

Ghoshte sat beside him, handing him a small knife. "For skinning," he said.

Casius took the blade, his hands steady despite the storm inside him. As he worked, Ghoshte's voice broke the quiet.

"Remember what I said. The forest is a battlefield. You're learning to fight it, but don't let it turn you into something else."

Casius nodded silently, the firelight casting shadows across his face. In his heart, he made a vow. He would find the bandits. He would stop them. And he would never forget the lessons of the hunt.

Chapter 20

Spring 1308 Garhelm Forest

The forest was quiet, its usual hum of life subdued under the hush of night. A faint breeze stirred the treetops, carrying the earthy scent of moss and damp leaves. The moon hung high, its silver glow spilling through the canopy and casting dappled patterns on the forest floor.

Marya stepped lightly along the trail, her bare feet brushing against the cool earth without a sound. She glanced back toward the cabin, its door shut tight, where Arla slept soundly beneath layers of blankets. Satisfied, she turned her attention to Althern, who followed a few steps behind her. His brow was furrowed slightly, curiosity evident in his expression.

"Where are we going?" he asked, his voice low but steady, as though unwilling to disturb the tranquillity around them.

"You'll see," Marya replied, a faint smile playing on her lips. The moonlight caught her eyes, making them glint like polished silver.

The path ahead was uneven, roots twisting and curling

like the fingers of ancient hands reaching through the soil. Marya moved effortlessly, her steps sure and practiced, while Althern's pace was more cautious. He avoided the roots and loose stones carefully, mindful of his still-healing wound. His hand pressed absently to his side, where the bandages were stiff beneath his tunic. Though the poison had long since been flushed from his body, thanks to Marya's skill with herbs, the scarred flesh still throbbed faintly with every motion.

"Are you all right?" Marya asked, glancing back at him.

Althern nodded, forcing a faint smile. "I've endured worse."

"Good," she said with a teasing smirk. "Because I don't plan on carrying you back."

Her playful remark caught him off guard, and he let out a quiet chuckle despite himself. She turned forward again, her pace quickening as they moved deeper into the forest. Althern followed, the faintest hint of a smile still on his lips.

The trail opened into a clearing, and there, nestled among the trees, was a small pond. Its surface gleamed like polished glass under the moonlight, reflecting the canopy above in fractured, silvery ripples. The air was cooler here, carrying the faint, clean scent of water that mingled with the earthy aroma of the woods.

Marya stepped forward, her face softening with quiet joy. "Isn't it beautiful?" she asked, her voice barely above a whisper, as though she feared disturbing the serene stillness of the scene.

Althern moved beside her, his gaze sweeping over the pond. "It is," he admitted, his voice gentler than usual. There was something about this place, its calmness, its isolation, that made his usual guarded demeanour slip, if only for a moment.

Marya stepped to the water's edge, letting her toes dip

into the shallows. The cool water sent a shiver up her spine, but she didn't seem to mind. Turning back toward Althern, her expression took on a playful edge.

"You're not afraid of a little water, are you?" she teased, raising an eyebrow.

Althern crossed his arms, giving her a bemused look. "Should I be?"

Marya grinned, reaching for the ties of her dress. "Only if you're afraid of getting in."

Before he could respond, she let the dress slip from her shoulders, revealing the smooth contours of her figure, illuminated by the soft, silvery glow of the moonlight. Her skin, pale and flawless, seemed to shimmer faintly, like the surface of the pond itself. The gentle curves of her body were accentuated by the play of light and shadow, creating an almost ethereal effect. Without hesitation, she stepped into the water, the cool ripples caressing her legs as she moved further in. Her movements were fluid and graceful, as if she were part of the night itself, merging seamlessly with water.

Althern quickly averted his gaze, his cheeks flushing. He fixed his attention on a nearby tree, his mind racing as he tried to gather his composure.

"Don't be shy, Althern," Marya called, her voice light with amusement. "Join me"

He hesitated, glancing back at her. She was floating lazily on her back now, her dark hair fanning out like a halo around her head. She looked so at ease, so free, that he felt a strange tug in his chest, something unfamiliar and unsettling. Slowly, he began removing his boots and pulling off his tunic, the bandage on his side stark against his skin. The cool night air prickled at his exposed body as he stepped toward the water.

"Come on," Marya urged, her laughter soft but insistent.

Althern waded in, the chill of the water biting at his skin

and sending a jolt up his spine. He hissed through his teeth, his muscles tensing as he adjusted to the temperature. Marya's laughter rang out again, a light, musical sound that seemed to melt some of his discomfort.

The water rose to their waists as they drifted toward the middle of the pond. The moon's reflection wavered between them, its pale light casting their faces in soft silver.

"You don't talk much, do you?" Marya said, breaking the silence. Her voice was gentle, though there was an undercurrent of curiosity.

Althern tilted his head, his lips curving into a faint smile. "Not much to say."

"I don't believe that" Marya said, wading closer to him. "You're always thinking about something. Always holding something back."

He shrugged, the motion causing a faint pull at his side. "Maybe."

Marya rolled her eyes and splashed water at him, catching him off guard. "You're impossible," she said with mock exasperation.

The unexpected splash drew a surprised laugh from him, the sound deep and warm. He shook his head, droplets of water dripping from his hair. "And you're relentless," he retorted, his tone lighter than before.

Her smile softened as she studied him, her expression shifting from playful to contemplative. "It's been a long time since you've laughed like that, hasn't it?" she asked gently.

Althern's smile faded slightly, and he nodded. "It has."

For a moment, neither of them spoke. The only sounds were the faint lapping of the water and the rustle of leaves in the breeze. Marya reached out, her fingers brushing lightly against his arm.

"I like this side of you," she said, her voice barely above a whisper.

Althern's breath hitched as her hand moved to his cheek, her touch warm despite the coolness of the water. Slowly, he leaned closer, their foreheads nearly touching.

"Marya…" he murmured, his voice unsteady.

She didn't let him finish. Closing the distance, her lips met his, soft and sure. For a moment, the world around them seemed to dissolve, leaving only the quiet intimacy of the moment.

They drifted back to the water's edge, their feet sinking into the cool grass. Under the rising moon, veiled by drifting clouds, they surrendered to the moment, letting the stillness of the forest hold them close.

Chapter 21

Spring 1308 Juntya Village

The sun had just begun to rise, spilling golden light over the forest as Grand Marshal Pesus stood at the edge of the camp, his breath misting in the morning air. Around him, the soldiers worked methodically to dismantle the makeshift fortifications they had built during their stay. The sounds of axes chopping, horses snorting, and men muttering carried on the cool breeze, mingling with the distant rustle of leaves.

Pesus was restless, his instincts prickling with unease. Something was wrong, though he couldn't quite place what. He was about to summon Captain Ghoshte when the thunder of hooves shattered the morning stillness.

A lone rider approached at breakneck speed, his cloak billowing behind him as his horse galloped toward the camp. Pesus strode forward to meet him, his posture straight and commanding. The courier dismounted with urgency, his face pale and drawn as he handed Pesus a sealed letter bearing the King's insignia.

"From His Majesty," the rider panted, his voice tight with exertion. "It's urgent."

Pesus broke the seal and unrolled the parchment, his sharp eyes scanning the letter. With each line, his jaw tightened, and a shadow passed over his face.

> *Grand Marshal Pesus,*
>
> *You are to return to Epiris at once with your men. Rok marches with an army from the northeast, intending to lay siege to our capital. The threat is dire, and we must bolster the city's defences immediately.*
>
> *Leave the border villages and forests to their fate for now. Epiris must not fall.*
>
> *By my command, Apius, King of Epiris.*

Pesus crushed the parchment in his fist, his lips pressed into a grim line as he turned back toward the camp. Ghoshte, Daka, and Bones were already striding toward him, their faces reflecting his concern.

"Rok's army is on the move," Pesus said, his tone clipped. "They're heading for Epiris. The King's orders are clear, we march home immediately."

"Rok?" Daka asked, his brow furrowing. "How many men?"

"It doesn't say," Pesus replied, his voice cold. "But if the King's calling every soldier back to defend the capital, it's more than just a rabble. This is war."

Before the captains could respond, a creaking sound drew their attention. A small cart trundled into camp from the direction of Juntya, pulled by a weary mule. Onboard were a middle-aged couple, their faces lined with exhaustion and worry. The man, stocky and broad shouldered, climbed down first, holding the reins tightly. The woman followed, clutching a scarf around her head to ward off the morning chill.

One of the soldiers moved to intercept them, but the couple waved him off striding past, their eyes scanning the camp with urgency. Pesus stepped forward, recognising the desperation etched into their faces.

"Grand Marshal," the man said, bowing stiffly. "We're looking for our son. His name's Pax. He left Juntya months ago to join the army. Have you seen him?"

Pesus' expression darkened, and he nodded slowly. "I know Pax."

The woman's face lit up with hope. "He's alive, then? Please, tell us where is he?"

Pesus hesitated, the weight of the truth bearing down on him. "Your son fought bravely," he began. "He was with the Prince's army when we liberated Juntya. But we were outnumbered, and Pax was captured by the enemy."

The woman gasped, her hand flying to her mouth as tears welled in her eyes. "Captured?" she whispered, her voice trembling.

The man's face hardened. "Who took him? Where?"

"Bandits," Pesus replied grimly. "Mercenaries, most likely. They could be working for Rok." He placed a firm hand on the man's shoulder, meeting his gaze with unwavering resolve. "Your son showed courage beyond his years. He stood his ground when others faltered. He's alive because of that courage. I swear to you i will see him returned."

The woman's quiet sobs broke the tense silence as she clung to her husband for support. "He's just a boy," she murmured.

The man swallowed hard, his voice thick with restrained

emotion. "He's strong. He'll hold on. But please, Marshal, bring him back to us."

Pesus nodded solemnly. "I will. You have my word. Your son is no ordinary soldier, he has a fire in him that I've rarely seen. I'll make sure he comes home."

The woman reached out, her trembling hand grasping Pesus' arm. "Thank you," she said softly, her voice breaking. "Please... bring my boy back."

Pesus straightened, his jaw tightening. "I will," he repeated, his tone unyielding. "No matter what it takes."

The army broke camp within the hour, the soldiers moving with grim efficiency as they began their march home. The air grew heavier as they neared the outskirts of Epiris, and the sight of smoke rising in the distance sent a chill through Pesus' veins.

By late afternoon, they crested a ridge overlooking the valley where the great walled city of Epiris stood. The sight that greeted them stopped Pesus in his tracks.

Rok's army had arrived.

Hundreds of soldiers surrounded the city in a sprawling encampment, their mix match of banners fluttering in the wind, mercenaries from around Rok's Kingdom. Siege engines loomed over the plain massive battering rams, catapults, and wooden towers poised to strike at the city walls.

Pesus' fists clenched as he surveyed the scene, his heart sinking. They were too late.

"We'll never get inside" Daka muttered, his voice grim.

Pesus didn't respond immediately, his eyes fixed on the city. The King's banners still flew defiantly above the highest tower, but smoke curled from the lower districts, and the faint sound of horns and drums carried on the wind, echoing through the valley.

"We hold position here," Pesus said at last, his voice

steady. "The King will know we're coming. We'll find a way."

The soldiers behind him murmured uneasily, their expressions a mix of fear and determination. Pesus turned to face them, his gaze sharp and commanding.

"Prepare for what's to come. We may be outnumbered, but we are not outmatched. Epiris will not fall while we stand."

The sun dipped lower in the sky, casting the valley in deep orange hues. As the shadows lengthened, Pesus stood on the ridge, his figure silhouetted against the fiery horizon. Below, Rok's banners whipped in the wind, their colours gleaming with cruel promise.

Pesus' thoughts drifted to Prince Althern, miles behind in Garhelm Forest, still weak from the poison that had nearly claimed his life. The burden of leadership felt heavier now, the path ahead darker.

Leadership is not glory, Pesus thought bitterly. It is a burden—a weight carried alone, the responsibility of deciding who lives, who fights, and who dies.

The first stars appeared in the darkening sky, twinkling faintly above the battlefield. Pesus took a deep breath, the cold night air sharp in his lungs.

"Rest while you can," he muttered, though the words were as much for himself as for his men. "Tomorrow, we fight."

Chapter 22

Spring 1308 Garhelm Forest
Marya's hut

Prince Althern awoke to the soft trill of birdsong filtering through the wooden shutters of Marya's hut. For a fleeting moment, he lay still, heavy with exhaustion, his chest rising and falling slowly. The ache in his shoulder, the lingering wound from the bandit's poisoned arrow—burned faintly, a constant reminder of how close he had come to death. Yet, for the first time in days, his thoughts were clear.

Turning his head, he saw Marya crouched by the hearth, coaxing the flames to life. She glanced over her shoulder, her lips curling into a faint smile.

"You're awake," she said softly. "How do you feel?"

Althern pushed himself up carefully, his muscles protesting the movement. He grimaced as pain flared in his shoulder.

"Like I've been trampled by a cavalry charge," he said with a dry chuckle. "But better than yesterday."

By the hearth, Arla sat cross-legged on the floor, carefully fletching an arrow. Her sharp, observant eyes flicked to him, scanning him critically.

"You don't look better," she said bluntly. "You still look pale."

Althern smirked faintly, shaking his head.

"I'll take your word for it, little one."

"Marya says the poison hasn't left you completely," Arla added matter of factly. "You shouldn't even be out of bed."

Marya shot her a sharp look, but Althern waved it off with a weak smile.

"She's not wrong," he admitted. "But I don't have the luxury of rest. I need to check on my men."

Swinging his legs over the edge of the bed, he paused as dizziness swirled through him. He braced himself for a moment, steadying his breath.

"You're stubborn, like all of them," Marya muttered, but there was no malice in her tone.

The path to the cavalry's camp wove through the dense, misty forest surrounding Marya's hut. The earthy scent of damp leaves filled the air, and shafts of sunlight pierced the canopy, dappling the ground with golden light. As Althern approached, the familiar sounds of camp life reached his ears —the snorts of restless horses, the clink of armour being adjusted, and the low murmur of conversation.

In a small clearing, his thirty cavalrymen were spread out, their mounts tethered to nearby trees. Though modest in number, these were men Althern trusted with his life—loyal soldiers who had followed him through skirmishes and battles.

Cavalryman Dren, the group's deputy leader, stepped forward as Althern entered the clearing. His sharp, weathered face broke into a smile.

"Your Highness," Dren said, bowing slightly. "It's good to see you up and walking."

There was a smile on Dren's face that Althern couldn't place.

"Walking might be generous," Althern replied wryly. "Stumbling is probably closer to the truth."

Dren chuckled, shaking his head. "Better than the state we brought you here in. Marya's done good work, keeping you breathing, maybe it's the swimming that's done you good."

Unable to help himself, Althern's face broke into a smile, he chose to ignore the comment and changed the subject.

"How are the men?" Althern asked, his gaze sweeping over the camp. Understanding the diversion, Dren continued.

"They're restless," He admitted. "Cavalrymen don't take well to sitting idle. They're used to action. But the horses are fed, the armour's polished, and they'll be ready to ride the second you give the order."

Althern nodded, his eyes settling on one of the horses—a tall black stallion with a gleaming coat that caught the morning light.

"Onyx looks fit," he said, a faint smile tugging at his lips.

Dren grinned. "That he is. But if you keep him waiting too long, he might throw you just to remind you who's in charge."

Althern chuckled lightly but said nothing. Though his mind felt clearer today, his body told a different story. The poisoned arrow had left its mark, and even small exertions sapped his strength.

"I'll speak to the men," Althern said after a pause.

Dren stepped aside as Althern moved to the centre of the clearing. The soldiers quickly gathered, their chatter falling silent as they turned their attention to him. Straightening his posture, Althern forced himself to stand tall despite the persistent ache in his shoulder.

"You've done well lingering in this camp," he began, his

voice steady but firm. "I know sitting in one place isn't easy for men like you, but your discipline is what keeps us strong. When the time comes, we'll ride out together, and we'll remind our enemies why the cavalry of Epiris is feared across these lands."

The men murmured in agreement, the tension in the clearing easing slightly. Althern could see it in their faces the unshakable faith they placed in him. It was a heavy burden, but one he had long since learned to carry.

"Stay sharp," he finished. "The forest isn't as quiet as it seems."

As the men returned to their tasks, Dren approached again, his voice low.

"Any word on when we'll move, Your Highness?"

"Not yet," Althern replied. "But soon."

The walk back to Marya's hut was slower, the morning's effort leaving Althern weary. The forest seemed quieter now, the sunlight filtering through the trees in shifting patterns.

Then he saw it.

A white wolf stood in the middle of the path, its fur shimmering faintly in the golden light. Its eyes bright, piercing gold, locked onto his, filled with an intelligence that sent a shiver down his spine.

Althern froze, his hand instinctively moving to his sword. But he stopped short, an unshakable sense washing over him. The creature wasn't hostile.

The wolf tilted its head, its gaze never leaving his. Then, without moving its mouth, it spoke.

"Your father needs you, Althern," the voice whispered, not aloud but in his mind. "Return to him before it's too late."

Althern's breath caught. He took a cautious step forward.

"Who sent you?" he demanded. "What are you?"

The wolf's ears twitched, and for a fleeting moment,

Althern thought he saw the faint outline of a woman's face overlaying its form.

"I am a guide," the wolf said. "Sent by those who see what you cannot. Go to your father, Prince, or the crown may fall."

Althern's chest tightened. "Tell me who sent you! And why me?"

The wolf's form shimmered, its edges dissolving like mist in the sunlight. Its golden eyes were the last to fade, hanging in the air as it spoke one final time.

"Because you are the son of a king... and the hope of what's to come."

And then it was gone.

By the time Althern reached Marya's hut, his mind was set. Marya was outside, hanging herbs to dry in the soft sunlight, while Arla played nearby, her laughter carrying through the still air.

"Marya," Althern called, his voice tight.

She turned, her smile fading as she caught sight of his expression.

"You're leaving," she said simply.

Althern nodded. "A wolf... it spoke to me. It said my father needs me. If I stay, it may be too late."

Marya's hands stilled, her grip tightening on the herbs she held.

"Amahra," she murmured. "The wolf deity who roams these lands. She's the mother of the forest."

Her eyes searched his face, her voice softening. "You're still weak, Althern. The wound hasn't fully recovered. If you ride now, you'll risk collapsing before you reach Epiris."

"I know" he said quietly. "But I have no choice."

Marya stepped closer, her voice trembling. "And what if you don't make it? What if you don't come back?"

Althern reached out, brushing a strand of hair from her face.

"I don't want to leave," he admitted. "But I must. My duty is to my father, to my kingdom. I can't turn my back on that."

For a long moment, Marya said nothing, her eyes searching his as though looking for a reason to make him stay. Finally, she sighed, her voice barely above a whisper.

"Then go. But promise me, you won't get yourself killed"

"I promise," Althern said, his voice steady despite the ache in his chest.

As Althern mounted his horse, the reins steady in his hands despite the lingering weakness in his limbs, his men gathered around him. Their faces were grim, their eyes sharp with resolve.

"We ride for Epiris," Althern said, his voice firm. "For the King."

The forest seemed to close behind them as they galloped southward, its shadows swallowing the memory of Marya's hut. But the wolf's words echoed in Althern's mind, driving him onward.

"Return before it's too late."

Chapter 23

Spring 1308 Garhelm Forest

Pax woke to the cold bite of the early morning air, his back aching from the uneven wooden planks beneath him. The rough wooden cage, mounted on the back of a creaking cart, shifted unsteadily with each lurch forward. His wrists stung with rope burns, the raw skin throbbing as he flexed his hands to bring back some feeling. Sunlight filtered through the dense canopy above, the beams of light dappling the forest floor in muted greens and golds.

He opened his eyes groggily, his thoughts muddled as he adjusted to his surroundings. Something felt off. Then it hit him—Felix was gone.

Panic surged through him, and he bolted upright, ignoring the sharp sting in his wrists. Scanning the cage desperately, he found no sign of the captain. The usual spot where Felix had sat, leaning against the rusted bars, was empty.

"Felix?" Pax croaked, his voice hoarse and dry.

There was no response, just the rhythmic crunch of boots on the forest trail and the low hum of voices from the guards walking alongside the cart. He turned his attention to the bandits, stationed lazily near the edge of the path. They were leaning against their weapons, their expressions indifferent as they shared muted jokes and swigs from a flask.

Pax's stomach tightened. Had Felix escaped? Or had the bandits done something to him during the night?

Before his thoughts could spiral further, one of the guards approached the cart, dragging Felix behind him. The captain's clothes were rumpled, and a fresh gash marred his cheek, but he was alive. Yet something about the way he walked, stiff and controlled, his shoulders tight—made Pax's unease deepen.

The guard shoved Felix roughly into the cage, slamming the door shut with a metallic clang. "Stay quiet, or next time it'll be worse," the guard snapped before retreating back to his comrades, his smirk lingering as if sharing a private joke.

"Felix!" Pax whispered, crawling to his side. "What happened? Where did they take you?"

Felix shifted to sit upright, wincing slightly. His face was pale, but his expression was hard to read—like a mask hastily put in place.

"Don't ask questions, boy," he muttered, his voice tight. "It's better if you don't know."

Pax frowned, unsure if the sharpness in Felix's tone was anger or something else. The captain's hand brushed over the fresh gash on his cheek, his fingers lingering there a moment.

Felix's gaze flicked briefly to the guards, then back to Pax. "Just focus on surviving," he said, softer now but no less tense. "That's all that matters."

Pax didn't press further. The shadow in Felix's eyes spoke volumes, though it wasn't a story the captain seemed willing to tell. Something gnawed at Pax, a sense that whatever had happened during the night had changed Felix. But whether for better or worse, he couldn't yet tell.

The cart jolted forward, the rough wheels creaking as it

rumbled along the uneven trail. Pax leaned against the rusted bars, watching the forest shift around them. The landscape had changed as they moved further south—dense greenery gave way to rocky outcroppings, and the air grew warmer and heavier.

Ahead, Widow and his men rode on horseback, their laughter and voices drifting back toward the cart. Though most of their words were lost in the distance, Pax caught enough fragments to piece together their destination: Epiris.

The name struck a chord deep within him. He had never seen the King's city, only heard of it in tales. Its towering walls, grand towers, and bustling streets had been described to him as a place of wonder. But now, the thought of being dragged there as a prisoner—used as a pawn in whatever scheme these mercenaries were concocting—filled him with dread.

"What do they want with me?" he murmured aloud.

Felix, who sat slumped against the bars, lifted his head. "You're leverage," he said grimly. "They think you're Prince Althern. And if they're dragging us to Epiris, it's because they mean to use you against the King."

"But I'm not the Prince!" Pax protested, his voice sharp.

"That doesn't matter to them," Felix said, his tone heavy with frustration. "What matters is what they can make the King believe."

By the time the cart crested a ridge overlooking the valley, Pax's breath caught in his throat.

Epiris.

The city rose against the horizon like a fortress carved from stone, its mighty walls standing proud and impenetrable. The tall towers that jutted skyward bore banners of royal blue and gold, their fabric snapping defiant in the wind. But the majesty of the sight was marred by what lay before it.

Rok's army.

The valley below was a sea of tents and banners, stretching across the plains. Siege engines loomed like dark sentinels, their jagged silhouettes stark against the bright sky. Smoke curled from countless campfires, and the distant hum of activity filled the air, the clanging of hammers, the crackle of fires, the shouts of officers giving orders.

Pax's stomach churned as the cart trundled down the slope, weaving through the outskirts of the camp. Soldiers turned to watch as the prisoners passed, their sharp eyes narrowing with suspicion and curiosity. Pax shrank back against the bars, his unease growing with every step closer to the heart of the enemy camp.

The cart came to a halt near a massive pavilion draped in emerald-green fabric, its size and elegance dwarfing everything around it. Widow dismounted from his horse, barking orders at his men as he gestured toward the cage.

"Stay quiet," Felix muttered, his voice barely audible.

Pax nodded, but his heart was pounding. Something drew his attention to the forest's edge beyond the encampment.

At first, it seemed like nothing more than a shadow among the trees. But as he looked closer, he saw it, a white wolf, its fur almost luminous in the dappled sunlight. Its golden eyes locked onto his, unblinking and piercing.

"Felix," Pax whispered, tugging at the captain's sleeve. "Do you see it?"

Felix followed his gaze but frowned. "See what?"

"The wolf," Pax said, his voice trembling. "It's watching us."

Felix squinted into the distance, then shook his head. "You're imagining things. Keep your head down, boy."

But Pax couldn't look away. The wolf remained perfectly still, its gaze unwavering. Then, as suddenly as it had appeared, it turned and slipped into the shadows of the forest, disappearing from sight.

Widow approached the cart, his polished armour gleaming in the sun despite the grime of the camp. His cold eyes swept over the prisoners, lingering on Pax.

"Well," Widow said with a smirk, "here we are. Epiris. You'll dine with your 'brother' tonight, Prince, before you play your part tomorrow."

The word "Prince" dripped with mockery, and Pax's stomach twisted with unease. There was something in Widow's gaze, a glint of amusement that chilled him to the bone.

The bandit leader unlocked the cage door and gestured for Pax to step out. Pax obeyed, his boots hitting the ground with a wet squelch. Thick mud splashed up Widow's pristine armour.

"You little fuck!" Widow snapped, his face darkening with fury.

Before Pax could react, Widow lashed out. His leg swept Pax's feet from under him, and the boy crashed into the mud with a heavy thud.

Cold water soaked through Pax's clothes as he struggled to push himself upright, but Widow was on him in an instant. Grabbing Pax by the throat, Widow pinned him to the ground, his grip like a vice.

Pax's lungs burned as he kicked and thrashed, but the slick mud offered no traction. His vision blurred, the edges darkening as his body screamed for air. From within the cage Felix barked. "ENOUGH, leave the boy. It was a mistake" Widow's face loomed above him, a cruel smile twisting his features.

"Don't die on me yet, 'Prince,'" Widow sneered. "I still need you alive for now."

Just as Pax's world teetered on the edge of unconsciousness, Widow released him. Pax collapsed into the mud, coughing and gasping for air as darkness threatened to pull him under. Widow stood over him, brushing mud from his armour with a look of disdain.

"Clean him up," Widow growled at one of his men. "He needs to look presentable for his royal reunion."

Pax lay motionless, his chest heaving as Widow's words echoed in his mind: "I still need you alive... for now."

Chapter 24

Spring 1308 Epiris

Pax's eyes snapped open, to the jarring sensation of being dragged, his back scraping along the rough ground. His head thudded against the earth with each step, the metallic taste of blood sharp in his mouth. Disoriented, he blinked up at the looming figure of Widow walking ahead, his broad shoulders silhouetted against the faint glow of scattered campfires. A soldier gripped Pax's ankles, pulling him through the dirt with an unceremonious determination.

The camp around them was alive with low murmurs and the clinking of metal. Makeshift tents swayed in the cold breeze, braziers crackled with faint orange light, and the smell of roasted meat hung in the air. Pax caught glimpses of mercenaries lounging by fires, their laughter muted and indifferent to his suffering.

He was dumped at the entrance of a large hide tent, his body crumpling like a discarded sack. Groaning, Pax rolled onto his side, his view tilting to reveal the interior of the tent: a long wooden table flanked by ornate chairs, its surface illuminated by the soft flicker of candlelight. The floor was lined with furs, and the warm glow of a brazier gave the space an air of eerie comfort.

A hand grabbed him by the scruff of his neck, hauling him to his feet. Widow's hot breath brushed Pax's ear as he leaned in, his voice low and dangerous.

"Time to play your part, boy."

Widow shoved him forward, guiding him roughly into the tent and forcing him into a chair at the far end of the table. Pax's eyes darted around the room. Against one wall, a chest sat open, revealing his armour and Felix's, along with his father's finely crafted blade glinting faintly in the light. The air was thick with the sweet, cloying scent of incense, mingling unpleasantly with the stale odour of sweat and mud.

Widow loomed at the other end of the table, his arms crossed and fingers drumming idly on his breastplate. His expression was a mask of smug satisfaction, his dark eyes glittering with malice.

Pax's pulse raced as he stared down at his bound wrists. He tried to think, tried to anticipate what was coming, but the oppressive heat of the room and Widow's unrelenting gaze left him feeling like a cornered animal.

"Where's Felix?" he demanded, his voice cracking. "What have you done to him?"

Widow's grin widened, exposing his teeth. "Don't worry about your captain. He's in good hands. Focus on yourself."

The sound of crunching gravel outside announced the arrival of King Rok. Widow stiffened, stepping back from the table, his posture straightening. The flap of the tent was thrown open, and the Eastern King entered, ducking slightly as he stepped inside.

Rok was a striking figure, but not in a way that inspired admiration. His dark hair was long and greasy, his posture slightly hunched, and his features bore a sharp resemblance to

Althern, but without his brother's nobility or charm. His presence radiated malice, his green eyes glinting with venomous hatred.

"So here we are, brother," Rok sneered, his voice dripping with disdain as he took his seat at the opposite end of the table. "It seems your loyalty to our father has bought you nothing but a slow and humiliating death. How poetic."

Pax's heart thundered in his chest, the blood roaring in his ears. He dared not speak, afraid that even the smallest word would betray the ruse.

Rok leaned forward, his lip curling. "Look at you, like a dog cowering before its master. I never understood why you were Father's favourite. Always the golden child. But where is he now, hmm? Is dear old King Apius coming to save you? Will he storm the camp tonight and carry you back to your throne?"

His voice rose, trembling with rage. "No. He sent you here to do his dirty work while he drowns himself in wine and women, just as he did when Mother was dying."

Rok slammed his fists against the table, the force sending a metal plate clattering to the floor. Pax flinched, his gaze darting to the King. For the briefest moment, he thought he saw something behind Rok's rage, a flicker of insecurity, of bitterness born from years of comparison.

But the moment was fleeting. Rok's attention turned sharply back to Pax, his expression darkening as he studied him more closely.

"Wait..." Rok murmured, his brow furrowing. "Who the fuck is this?"

Rok's chair scraped loudly against the floor as he rose, his eyes narrowing in suspicion.

"That's not my—"

The final word never left his lips. Widow moved like a

striking viper, his hand darting beneath his cloak to retrieve a hidden blade. In a single, fluid motion, he plunged the knife into Rok's throat.

The King's eyes widened in shock, his hands flying to his neck as blood spurted in thick, crimson arcs. A guttural choking sound escaped his lips as he staggered backward, his body hitting the floor with a heavy thud.

Pax watched in horror as Widow followed the King's collapsing form, driving the blade into Rok's chest again and again. The sickening sound of metal meeting flesh filled the room, each strike sending splatters of blood across the furs and Widow's armour.

When it was over, Rok lay still, his lifeless eyes staring blankly at the ceiling. Widow straightened, wiping the blade on a nearby cloth with a casual air.

"Stand up," Widow ordered, his voice low and urgent.

Pax hesitated, his body frozen with shock. Widow grabbed his arm, hauling him to his feet. Before Pax could react, the bandit leader pulled him into a tight embrace, smearing Rok's blood across his clothes.

Stepping back, Widow slashed the bonds on Pax's wrists and pressed the bloodied blade into his trembling hand.

"Hold it," Widow hissed.

Pax stared down at the knife, his stomach churning as the sticky warmth of the blood seeped into his skin. He opened his mouth to protest, but Widow didn't give him the chance.

"GUARDS!" Widow bellowed, his voice carrying through the camp. "The prisoner, he's armed!"

A short delay before the tent flap burst open as nearby guards stormed inside, their eyes widening at the scene before them. For a moment, they hesitated, their shock rendering them immobile.

Then they sprang into action.

Swords drawn, they rushed Pax, tackling him to the ground. He didn't resist as they bound his wrists and ankles once more, the knife clattering uselessly to the floor.

Pax's gaze flicked to Widow, who stood calmly amidst the chaos, his expression unreadable. Their eyes met, and for a fleeting second, Pax thought he saw a glint of triumph in Widow's gaze.

Later that night, Pax lay in the cage once more, his body aching from the guards' rough handling. Felix sat nearby, his face grim as he studied the boy.

"What happened?" Felix asked quietly.

Pax shook his head, unable to find the words. The image of Rok's lifeless eyes and the weight of the knife in his hand played over and over in his mind.

Back in the tent, Widow stood alone, his lips curling into a satisfied smile. The plan had worked. With Rok dead, he now commanded the largest army in Valhelm. By morning, the camp would be united in fury, and the boy's public execution would fuel their lust for blood.

Widow turned to one of the guards. "Prepare the gallows at dawn, in full view of Epiris. Let the King see what's coming for him."

He reached into his tunic, producing a sealed letter. "Send this to Apius. Let's see how much he's willing to sacrifice for his son."

As the guard departed, Widow stepped outside, inhaling the crisp night air. The camp was already alive with whispers of betrayal and vengeance.

This was only the beginning. Epiris would fall, and the throne would soon be his.

Chapter 25

Spring 1308 Epiris

Pax lay awake, staring at the stars scattered across the night sky, their faint glow barely visible through the gaps in the thick tree canopy. Sleep eluded him. Felix had listened to his retelling of Widow's treachery, nodding absently, but something about the captain's distant expression had unsettled Pax. Shortly after, Felix had turned over and fallen into a restless sleep, leaving Pax alone with his thoughts.Now the wheels were in motion and Pax knew no way to stop them.

Tomorrow, they were to face execution, a certainty that gnawed at Pax's mind. He tried to push the thought away, but his imagination betrayed him, conjuring images of the gallows and the leering faces of their enemies.

His mind drifted back to Juntya, to home. He pictured his father at the forge, his face weathered but kind, patient even when Pax made mistakes. His chest tightened with guilt. He wished he could see them one last time, to apologise for leaving without saying goodbye, for thinking he could lighten the family's burden by joining the army. He blinked away the tears forming in his eyes, but the effort was futile. Warm trails ran down his cheeks, glistening in the faint light. He muffled his sobs as he broke, racked with guilt, alone, facing his death tomorrow.

Angry at himself for giving in to despair, Pax rolled onto his side, trying to block out the sounds around him. The camp was eerily quiet, save for the faint murmur of voices and the low crackle of dying braziers. For the past hour, the rhythmic sounds of sawing and hammering had filled the air. He didn't need to ask what they were building, the gallows that would end his life were taking shape only two hundred paces away.

Pax felt utterly alone. What had he done to deserve such a cruel end? How had he become entangled in this web of lies and betrayal? Widow's manipulation was as cunning as it was ruthless. Pax now understood that the bandit leader had always known he wasn't Althern, but he had used Pax's identity to further his twisted schemes.

A group of guards passed nearby, their boots crunching softly on the dirt. Pax ignored them, closing his eyes in a futile attempt to will himself to sleep. Moments later, a low, familiar voice broke the silence.

"Oi, you coming or what?"

Pax's eyes snapped open, his heart racing. Pressed against the bars of the cage was a boy in a green cloak, Casius. The sight of him brought a flood of relief. Casius grinned when he saw Pax's astonished expression.

"Thought we'd best pull you out of this mess before you got your head chopped off," Casius said, his tone light despite the danger.

Behind him loomed Ghoshte, the archer captain. His sharp features were tense, his eyes darting around to scan the camp. "Casius, get the door untied," he ordered in a low growl.

Casius pulled out a hunting knife and began sawing at the

rope securing the cage door. Within moments, the knot gave way, and the door swung open with a soft creak. Casius climbed inside and set to work on Pax's bindings.

"That's a fine blade," Pax muttered as the ropes around his wrists fell away. "You'll have to show me if we get out of here alive."

Casius smirked. "Deal."

Felix stirred, sitting up with a bewildered look on his face as he registered what was happening. Pax slid out of the cage, his bare feet sinking into the cold, damp ground. The mud clung to him, but he didn't care, freedom, even tentative, was intoxicating.

"Let's go," Ghoshte whispered, motioning for Felix to follow. The captain hesitated only briefly before jumping down.

"My blade and armour" Felix said urgently. "They're in a tent just a few paces from here. Can we get them?"

Ghoshte cursed under his breath. "We ran out of time before we even entered the camp. Dawn's almost upon us."

Relenting with a sigh, Ghoshte threw cloaks to Pax and Felix. "Fine. Show me where."

The group moved silently through the camp, their footsteps muffled on the soft grass. Ahead, the tent where the King's body lay loomed. A lone guard sat outside on a log, chewing on a piece of meat, his head nodding sleepily.

Ghoshte cleared his throat as he approached. "Guard change. Orders from the top. You can get some rest."

Before the man could respond, Ghoshte lunged, clamping a hand over his mouth and dragging him into the tent. A muffled struggle ended with a sickening crunch. Pax stepped through the flap just in time to see the guard's body crumple to the floor.

The chest sat where it had been earlier, its contents

untouched. Pax moved quickly, securing his armour and sword. His fingers trembled slightly as he adjusted the straps, the familiar weight of the blade in his hand grounding him.

"Pax" Ghoshte said quietly, nodding toward the table. "Is that who I think it is?"

Pax glanced at the shrouded body of Rok, wrapped in a white sheet. "Yeah. I'll fill you in when we're sitting by a friendly campfire."

Felix, now armed, stepped out into the cool night air. He nodded at Ghoshte, a faint smile breaking his otherwise grim expression. "Good to see you've still got all your limbs, brother."

Ghoshte smirked. "Same to you, Felix. Now let's move."

The group, Ghoshte, three of his men, Felix, Pax, and Casius, slipped deeper into the camp. The moonlight was faint, but enough to guide them through the maze of tents and sleeping bodies. Occasionally, they passed men huddled by low burning fires, but most of the camp was quiet.

A voice grumbled nearby, making the group freeze.

"Where you off to?"

Pax's breath hitched, his muscles tensing. The man who had spoken lay on his side, his eyes closed.

"Ah, you ignorant fuck..." the voice mumbled.

Pax exhaled slowly, realising the man was talking in his sleep. He motioned for Ghoshte to keep moving, and they continued, their footsteps even softer now.

At the camp's edge, two guards stood watch, their silhouettes stark against the faint glow of a distant fire. Suddenly, the clatter of metal rang out behind them. Pax turned to see Felix withdrawing his foot from a spilled brazier. The embers rolled against a leather tent, igniting instantly.

"Shit" Felix hissed, stomping at the grass to wipe his boot.

The flames licked hungrily at the tent, quickly spreading. Nearby bodies stirred, groaning and shifting as the firelight grew brighter.

"Well" Felix muttered, drawing his sword, "if they didn't know we were here before, they do now."

The guards rushed toward the commotion, swords drawn. Pax stepped forward, swinging his blade in a wide arc. One guard raised his arm to block, only for Pax's strike to sever it cleanly. The man collapsed with a piercing cry, Pax's blade plunging into his stomach to finish the job.

Casius faced the other guard, sidestepping his clumsy attack. Quick and precise, the boy drove his hunting knife into the man's gut, dragging it upward with all his strength. Warm blood splashed over Casius's hand as the guard crumpled.

"Run!" Ghoshte barked.

Adrenaline surging, the group bolted for the forest. The crackling fire and shouts of the waking camp faded behind them as they plunged into the trees.

When they were deep in the woods, Ghoshte held up a hand, signalling a halt. His keen eyes scanned the darkness, searching for signs of pursuit. The others stood hunched, panting from the exertion.

"I left twelve of my archers hidden in the treeline," Ghoshte muttered, his voice grim. "They're gone. Either captured or dead."

He turned to the group, his expression hard. "From here on, this is enemy ground. Stay sharp. We move silently, single file. Let's go."

The party nodded, their resolve steeling as they followed Ghoshte into the shadows of the forest, their steps swallowed by the silence of the trees.

Chapter 26

Spring 1308 Woodland overlooking
Epiris

The sound of a battle horn shattered the eerie stillness of the woodland. Ghoshte motioned toward the direction of the enemy camp, his expression grim.

"Looks like your absence has been noticed."

Casius, wide-eyed, stared back toward the distant glow of fires flickering through the trees. The forest felt suffocatingly close, the humid air heavy around them. Earlier, Ghoshte had led them off the main trail onto a narrow animal track, but in the thick darkness, finding it again seemed impossible.

The seven of them crept forward, each step painfully loud. The snap of a twig or the crunch of leaves underfoot felt like a thunderclap in the unnatural silence. Even the usual rustling of forest creatures had stilled, as though the woodland itself held its breath. Ghoshte suddenly raised a clenched fist, motioning for them to halt.

They crouched low, scanning the shadowy expanse ahead. At first, Casius heard nothing but the blood pounding in his ears. Then, faintly, the sound of jingling metal drifted through the trees, followed by the murmur of distant voices.

Ghoshte's whisper carried back through the group. "Search party. Stay quiet and let them pass."

The tension crackled in the air as the voices grew louder, accompanied by the rhythmic crunch of boots on the forest floor. Casius strained to listen, trying to count the footsteps to gauge their numbers, but the sounds overlapped, impossible to separate. It was more than they had, that much he knew.

Torches flickered into view. At first, they looked like distant fireflies, their glow bobbing and weaving through the trees. But as the search party drew nearer, the light grew stronger, the flames casting ominous shadows across the undergrowth. Casius counted at least twelve torches.

A sudden loud snap to their right made Casius flinch. His breath caught as he froze in place, willing himself to blend into the foliage. The voices of the search party became sharper, closer. The torches, now no more than twenty paces away, illuminated the faint outlines of the men.

Ghoshte nocked an arrow, the faint creak of the bowstring breaking the silence. He glanced at Casius, nodding once, urging him to do the same. Casius obeyed, his hands trembling as he drew back his bowstring, his eyes fixed on the nearest torch. Down the line, the other three archers followed suit, their movements precise and silent.

There was no way out. The forest was too dense to run, and the enemy surrounded them. Ghoshte raised his hand, counting down with his fingers. Five... four... three... Casius's heart hammered in his chest as he aimed at the torchbearer second from the right. Two... one...

The arrows flew in unison, their sharp hiss cutting through the air. A chorus of startled screams erupted as the arrows found their marks. Several men collapsed, their bodies crumpling like broken marionettes.

Casius swiftly nocked another arrow, his eyes darting to

Ghoshte for direction. The captain had already begun advancing through the ferns, his bow trained on the shifting shadows ahead. Casius followed, stepping carefully over roots and foliage, his body tense and ready to fire again.

As they moved forward, Pax dispatched the wounded enemies lying on the forest floor, their groans silenced by quick thrusts of his blade. The remaining torches ahead hadn't moved. Casius found this strange, the men holding them had made no attempt to retreat or regroup despite the chaos.

When they reached the edge of the woodland, the reason became clear. The torchbearers stood motionless, deliberately still, their faces shadowed by the flickering flames. At their centre stood Widow, his tall frame illuminated by the glow of the fire. His smug grin was a beacon of malevolence.

"It's a trap!" Ghoshte hissed. "We're being surrounded!"

Before anyone could react, men emerged from the trees behind them, their weapons glinting faintly in the torchlight. They moved with practiced efficiency, forming a semi-circle to cut off the group's escape.

Ghoshte spun to face the new threat but was immediately struck down by the hilt of a massive soldier's sword. The captain crumpled to the ground, unconscious.

Casius turned his attention back to Widow, his vision narrowing with rage. Memories of his mother's death in Niborya flooded his mind. Her screams, Widow's laughter, the blood that stained the ground. His chest burned with fury. This was his chance.

His hands steadied as he raised his bow, the string taut as he took aim at Widow's chest. The bandit leader hadn't moved, his smug confidence unwavering. Casius exhaled and released the arrow.

The shot struck Widow's breastplate with a metallic

clang, glancing off harmlessly. Widow's grin faltered for the briefest moment, his eyes narrowing in irritation before his voice boomed across the clearing.

"Seize them! No more fucking heroics!"

The group was quickly disarmed, their weapons snatched away as they were shoved into a line. The soldiers herded them out of the forest and into the open ground. Widow stood before them, gloating as though he were addressing a group of unruly children.

"You know," he said, his tone mocking, "it's incredibly rude to leave without saying goodbye."

He paced in front of them, his hands clasped behind his back. His gaze lingered on Pax, his eyes gleaming with malice. "Especially you, Prince. Big day tomorrow."

Widow gave an exaggerated bow, his grin widening as he spun on his heel and stalked away, leaving the prisoners under heavy guard.

Each step back toward Widow's camp felt like a lead weight in Casius's chest. The failure stung like an open wound. He had let his emotions cloud his judgement, just as Ghoshte had warned him not to. Now they were captives once more.

Ghoshte, his head bowed and blood trickling from his temple, glanced back at Casius and gave a small, reassuring nod. It was a gesture of solidarity, a quiet reminder to stay strong. But even that was cut short as one of the guards shoved the archer captain forward.

From somewhere in the forest, a sharp whistle pierced the air. A sound so faint that Casius barely registered it. Ghoshte, however, tensed immediately before relaxing again, his steps steady and deliberate.

As they neared the clearing where they had first entered the woods, Ghoshte suddenly slowed, earning irritated shoves from the guards behind him. The third shove sent him sprawling to the ground, his face hitting the dirt.

Ghoshte sucked in a painful breath before shouting with all his might. "Down! NOW!"

Before Casius could process the words, Pax slammed into him, forcing him to the ground. A fraction of a second later, the air filled with the hiss of arrows.

The enemy guards dropped like stones, their cries of pain drowned out by the chaos. Casius gasped for air, the weight of Pax pinning him down.

"The whistle," Pax whispered urgently. "It's the same one Ghoshte used before. Didn't you notice?"

Casius shook his head, his admiration for Pax's quick thinking growing.

Figures emerged from the treeline, Ghoshte's missing archers, their bows still drawn. From deeper in the woods came the thunder of hooves as cavalry burst into the clearing.

The horses stamped and snorted, their riders shining like wraiths in the moonlight. At the centre of the formation, a rider dismounted, his mud covered armour catching the faint glow of the moonlight.

"Surround them," the rider commanded, his voice calm but unyielding. His men formed a protective circle around the captives and the remaining enemies.

Pax's eyes widened in recognition. "It's Althern!"

The boy's grin spread across his face as the Prince strode forward, drawing his sword with a sharp metallic ring.

"Can't let you have all the fun, can I?" Althern said, his voice cutting through the tension like a blade.

Chapter 27

Spring 1308 Woodland Overlooking Epiris

Althern's men stood in silence, their swords drawn and held low, forming a tight circle around the clearing. Firelight from nearby torches flickered across their faces, casting long shadows that danced across the trees. The stillness was broken only by the distant chirping of crickets and the quiet hum of restless men awaiting their Prince's command.

Althern stepped into the centre of the clearing, his sword steady despite the dull ache in his shoulder. Across from him, Widow smirked, leaning casually on his blade.

Widow's gaze swept over the soldiers surrounding him. "Quite the turnout for such a little show," he mocked. "Do you really think this ends here, Althern? You might kill me, but my men will cut through yours like wolves through sheep."

Althern raised his sword, his voice calm and resolute. "No one else dies tonight. This is between us."

Widow chuckled, pushing himself upright and pacing a few steps closer. "Between us? That's rich. You can barely stand without wincing. Tell me, Prince, are you planning to win this duel with sheer determination alone?"

Althern didn't reply, raising a hand to signal his men to hold their ground.

Widow tilted his head, his grin widening. "You think this will save lives, don't you? One noble duel to spare the bloodshed. But you've already lost one brother to me. I don't mind adding another to the tally."

The words hit Althern like a blow. His grip on the hilt of his sword slackened briefly. "What are you talking about?"

Widow's smirk turned into a predatory grin. "Oh, haven't you heard? Poor Prince Rok. He died with my blade in his throat. And let me tell you, he wasn't nearly as noble as the ballads make him sound."

Althern's chest tightened, his blood turning cold. While Rok had betrayed their father and attacked Epiris to claim the throne for himself, the news of his death still struck deep. Memories of their childhood flashed through Althern's mind, training together, sparring in the castle courtyard, running through the halls as boys.

"You're lying," Althern said, his voice low but trembling with restrained fury.

"Am I?" Widow replied, circling slightly, his words dripping with malice. "You'll know the truth soon enough, assuming you live long enough to ask him in the afterlife."

Althern steadied his grip on his sword. The fire in his chest surged, chasing away the shock. "If what you say is true, then you've just signed your own death warrant."

He lunged first, his blade slicing through the air towards Widow's chest. Widow sidestepped smoothly, bringing his sword up to parry. The clash of steel rang out through the clearing as the two began circling each other, their movements careful and calculated, each testing the other's resolve.

Widow struck next, a sweeping slash aimed at Althern's side. The Prince twisted, narrowly avoiding the blow and countering with a sharp thrust. Widow dodged again, grinning.

"You're not bad," Widow taunted, his voice laced with mockery. "But I can see it, the drag in your step, the weight in your arm. That wound is slowing you down, isn't it?"

Althern gritted his teeth and pressed forward, forcing Widow to retreat with a flurry of quick strikes. His movements were precise, but his speed was failing him. Each swing sent a sharp pull through his injured shoulder, the throbbing pain worsening with every attack.

Widow saw it.

He darted in low, his blade cutting towards Althern's thigh. The Prince parried, but the force of the blow nearly unbalanced him. Widow followed with a lunge, slicing through Althern's sleeve and drawing a thin line of blood along his arm.

"Sloppy" Widow sneered, laughing as he stepped back. "I've already killed one prince. Let's make it two."

Althern ignored the taunts, summoning his strength for a powerful overhead swing. Widow blocked, his knees bending under the force, but he recovered quickly, slipping out of Althern's reach with ease.

The men surrounding the clearing watched with grim silence, their knuckles tight on their swords. Pax, standing on the edge of the circle, felt his pulse pounding in his ears. He gripped the hilt of his blade, the one Althern had given him, forged by his father's hands. The weight of the weapon felt heavier than ever, but its balance was perfect.

He couldn't stand by and watch any longer. Althern was faltering, his breathing ragged, his movements slower with each strike. Widow's jeering voice seemed to fuel Pax's anger.

Without thinking, Pax stepped into the circle, raising his blade.

"Stay back!" Althern's voice rang out sharply, though it lacked its usual strength.

Pax ignored him. He charged, his sword descending in a powerful arc. Widow turned just in time to block, the impact forcing him to stagger back a step.

"Another little hero" Widow sneered. "Let's see if you're as useless as the last prince I killed."

Pax pressed the attack, his strikes clumsy but relentless. Widow's grin faltered as he was forced to defend himself. Pax's raw determination caught him off guard.

"You've got fire, I'll give you that" Widow spat, lunging forward. Pax ducked under the swing and countered with a thrust, the blade slicing into Widow's arm. Blood dripped onto the ground as Widow hissed in pain.

Pax raised his blade for a finishing blow, his heart racing.

Steel met steel.

Pax blinked in confusion, his sword locked against another.

"Felix?" His voice cracked with disbelief.

Felix stood before him, his blade raised to intercept the strike. His face was unreadable, cold.

"Step back" Felix ordered, his tone low and firm.

Althern staggered to his feet, his expression a mix of pain and fury. "What are you doing?"

Widow chuckled from behind Felix, wiping the blood from his arm. "Oh, they don't know. Keeping secrets, are we, Felix?"

Felix said nothing, his stance unwavering.

"What did he promise you?" Althern demanded, his voice

raw with betrayal. "What's worth turning against your Prince?"

Widow smirked. "He doesn't have to explain himself. But I will say, he's been... useful. Isn't that right, Felix?"

Felix's jaw tightened, his knuckles whitening around the hilt of his sword. He glanced at Widow, his expression hardening further. "Shut up" he said coldly before turning his gaze to Althern.

"You want to know why, Althern?" Felix's voice wavered, not with weakness but with barely restrained anger. "Because loyalty only gets you so far. I bled for this kingdom. I fought in battles you'll only ever read about. I trained men who would have died for me without question. But when it came time to name a Grand Marshal, when it came time to choose someone who actually *earned* it, they picked Pesus."

He spat the name as though it burned his tongue.

"They wanted the safe choice," Felix continued, his voice rising. "The obedient one. The one who'd follow orders without question. And what did I get for my years of service? A pat on the back and orders to kneel to my equal!"

Althern's eyes narrowed, his breathing laboured but steady. "You think this justifies treason? Betraying the men you fought beside, the people you swore to protect?"

Felix scoffed, his grip on his sword tightening. "I've done more protecting than you ever will. I've seen what this kingdom does to people like me, people who speak up, who see the cracks. It chews us up and spits us out, and for what? To protect a legacy built on lies and corruption?"

Widow stepped closer, his grin widening, relishing in the pain Althern was feeling. "Well said, Felix. It's a shame they never listened to you."

Felix shot him a glare, his lips curling, before refocusing on Althern. "You're not ready to rule, Althern. You're too soft, too idealistic. You think you can hold this kingdom together with words and promises? Power doesn't work like that. It takes action. Ruthlessness."

"And you think Widow is the answer?" Pax interjected, his voice trembling with disbelief. "You'd rather follow *him*?"

Felix hesitated for the briefest moment, his gaze flickering. "Widow's not perfect" he admitted, his tone begrudging. "But at least he's willing to do what needs to be done. He's not clinging to some naïve dream of unity."

Althern's expression darkened, his voice cutting through the tension. "And what about honour, Felix? What about the men who trusted you? Does that mean nothing to you anymore?"

Felix's eyes flashed with anger, but beneath it was something deeper—regret, perhaps, or pain. "Honour doesn't fill your belly. It doesn't rebuild cities or protect the people who've been forgotten. Sometimes, you have to make choices you don't want to make. But you wouldn't understand that, would you?"

He took a step back, lowering his blade slightly but keeping it ready. "Step aside, Althern. This isn't your fight anymore."

The clearing erupted into chaos as Widow's men surged forward, breaking the circle. Steel clashed against steel, and the air filled with shouts and the screams of the wounded.

Pax fought like a man possessed, his blade finding its mark as he defended Althern. The Prince, bloodied but unrelenting, pushed himself forward, desperate to reach Felix. But the press of fighting held him back.

Through the chaos, Felix and Widow slipped away,

retreating toward the forest. Widow glanced back, his grin gleaming in the firelight.

"I'll take care of Felix, Althern" he called. "He's earned his place."

Felix hesitated for a fraction of a second, his eyes meeting Althern's. Then, without a word, he turned and disappeared into the shadows.

When the last of Widow's men were subdued or had fled, the clearing fell silent. Althern collapsed to one knee, his injuries finally taking their toll.

Pax stood nearby, his blade dripping with blood, his hands trembling as the weight of what had happened began to sink in.

"Felix..." Althern murmured, his voice hollow.

"He's gone," Pax said bitterly. "He let Widow escape. He betrayed us."

Althern nodded slowly, his expression darkening. "Felix will answer for this," he said, his voice cold as steel.

He turned to Pax, placing a hand on his shoulder. "You fought well. Better than some of my knights. Thank you."

Still distracted by Felix's betrayal, Althern walked away. Pax stood in silence, staring at the blood on his blade, the blade his father had forged.

The memory of Felix's return after being dragged from the cage struck him. Felix had been bloodied but silent, refusing to say what had happened. Now it was clear, he hadn't been tortured. He had been recruited.

As the sun began to rise, bathing Epiris in a soft orange glow, Pax felt the weight of his actions settle on him. He had fought, killed, and survived. But Widow's mocking laughter still echoed in his mind.

This isn't over.

Chapter 28

Spring 1308 Rok's Camp

The camp was quiet, save for the crackle of the fire and the distant rustle of the forest beyond. Felix sat on a low log, his head bowed, his hands clasped tightly together. His sword rested against his knee, its hilt still slick with blood. The echoes of the battle clung to him, clashing steel, the cries of the dying, and the sickening moment when his blade deflected Pax's strike from Widow.

He hadn't wanted to stop it. But he had.

From the shadows, Widow emerged, his steps light yet deliberate. His sharp eyes gleamed in the firelight, his ever-present smirk playing at the corners of his mouth. His coat was flecked with ash, and a faint smear of dried blood marked his collar, but he was otherwise untouched.

"Felix" Widow said, his voice soft, almost affable. "You made quite the impression back there."

Felix glanced up, his jaw tight. "I wasn't exactly looking to impress."

Widow's smirk widened as he lowered himself onto the log opposite Felix. He leaned forward, resting his elbows on his knees, his posture casual but his gaze piercing. "And yet you did. Stopping that boy's blade from ending me, that wasn't just a decision, Felix. It was a statement."

Felix's grip tightened on his sword. "It wasn't for you," he muttered.

"Ah, but it was," Widow countered smoothly. "You may not want to admit it, but you chose a side. And you chose right."

Felix's laugh was sharp, bitter. "Right? I betrayed my king, Widow. My men, my honour, everything I've stood for, gone. Forgive me if I don't feel like celebrating."

Widow's smile faltered for a moment, replaced by a calculating look. "What you stood for, Felix, was a lie. You were loyal to a boy waiting for his chance with the crown You saw the cracks, didn't you? In Althern's rule, in his decisions. And yet you stayed loyal to the end. Until now."

Felix's gaze dropped to the fire, the flickering flames reflecting in his tired eyes. "Maybe Althern wasn't ready. But that doesn't mean you're the answer."

Widow chuckled, the sound low and amused. "You're right, I'm not the answer. I'm the disruption. The storm that clears the rot away. Althern plays at being wanna-be King, but a kingdom doesn't need a boy with ideals. It needs strength. Purpose. Direction. King Apius is too out of touch to care"

Felix's knuckles whitened around the hilt of his sword. "And you think you're strong enough to rule?"

"Rule?" Widow leaned back, his smirk returning. "Oh no, Felix. I'm not here to wear a crown. That's for men like you. Once Epiris is mine, you'll take the throne. The people will follow a warrior, someone they can respect. Rok's army will march south with me, whilst I claim the lands of the Brotherhood, and build my own dominion. I'll ensure that both kingdoms thrive under our shared banner."

Felix's eyes narrowed, his wariness returning. "So that's it? I get Epiris and you... what? Pull the strings from the shadows?"

Widow's grin widened, his teeth glinting in the firelight. "Precisely. Ruling is a tedious game, Felix. Petitions, taxes, squabbling nobles, I've no patience for it. But guiding kings? Shaping empires? That, I think i could excel at."

Felix shook his head, his expression darkening. "You talk like this is all inevitable, like the pieces will fall into place just because you want them to. But you're not as untouchable as you think. One day, someone will come for you."

Widow tilted his head, unbothered by the warning. "Perhaps. But by then, you'll have your crown, and I'll have my lands. Tell me, Felix, if not me, who else could have made this happen? Who else could break the chains holding this kingdom back?"

Felix didn't answer immediately. He thought of Althern, of Pesus, of the life he'd left behind. He thought of the sting of being passed over for Grand Marshal, the years of loyalty that had earned him little more than obscurity. Widow's words struck a nerve, but they didn't sit comfortably.

"I didn't do this for power," Felix said finally, his voice low but firm. "I didn't join you to be a pawn in your game."

Widow's expression softened, though his eyes remained sharp. "No, Felix, you joined me because you knew the old ways were broken. Althern clung to a failing system, one that chewed up men like you and spat them out. I'm not asking for your trust, or your devotion. I'm asking for your resolve. Together, we'll build something better. Something stronger."

Felix's jaw tightened, his thoughts a storm of doubts and regrets. He thought of the men who had followed him into battle, the bonds forged in blood and fire. He thought of the boy who had once trusted him with his life, now cast aside like a broken blade.

Widow rose to his feet, brushing ash from his coat. "You've made your choice, Felix. And it was the right one. You don't have to see it yet. But one day, you'll look back and realise I gave you everything you ever wanted. A kingdom of your own. A chance to rule instead of being ruled over."

Felix said nothing as Widow disappeared into the shadows, his steps fading into the night.

The fire crackled softly, casting flickering patterns on Felix's face. He stared into the flames, the heat brushing against his skin but failing to warm him. He didn't feel like a king. If anything, he felt like a man who had lost himself, trapped in a web of promises and manipulation.

The fire burned on, but the shadows felt darker than before.

CHAPTER 29

SPRING 1308 EPIRIS KINGS HALL

King Apius stood at the edge of the city's battlements, his eyes narrowing as they scanned the distant hills. The assault had come without warning. One moment, he had been preparing for the execution of his son; the next, his army was forced to lurch into motion, rushing to defend the city gates. The banners flying under the enemy's assault were unmistakable, Rok's. His son's.

Apius hadn't been given weeks to prepare, not even days. This was a calculated strike borne of opportunism, and the King knew it. But he would not allow it to succeed.

Straightening his shoulders, he stifled the ache that settled deep in his bones. At sixty, the weight of rule and war pressed heavily upon him. Every breath came with effort; every motion reminded him of how much his body had endured. Yet, for all his age, Apius had not lost the fire of command. He'd faced worse before, and this, too, would pass, one way or another.

At first light, Apius had ridden through the streets of Epiris. The fear in the air was palpable, clinging to the city like mist. The people had parted nervously as his horse clattered over the cobblestones, their murmurs low, their faces pale. They were right to be afraid. War was upon them. But as Apius passed, he felt no pity for their unease. Fear was necessary. It was a reminder of the stakes, a reminder of the cost of peace.

Now, as the tremors of the enemy's approach shook the ground beneath the walls, Apius's heart pounded. The sun hung low in the sky, casting long shadows over the defences of Epiris. The morning sun shone glinting off the soldiers armour.

The drums began first, their low, rhythmic pounding drifting across the plains. The enemy's cries followed soon after, rising in a terrible cacophony. Apius could see their forces assembling on the horizon, a tidal wave of men and siege engines bristling with deadly intent.

Behind him, his soldiers stood in rows along the battlements. Their faces were grim, their knuckles white as they gripped their weapons. Fear lingered in their eyes, but it wasn't the fear that broke men, it was the fear that sharpened resolve. And today, Apius needed their resolve.

He turned to face them, his voice rising to cut through the heavy tension.

"Soldiers of Epiris!" he began, his tone a sharp edge honed by years of war. "Today, we stand not just as men, but as the last bastion of this kingdom. We are the blood of those who fought before us, the fathers, the brothers, the sons who laid down their lives to defend this land."

He paced along the wall, his armour gleaming faintly in the sunlight. These were not strangers to him. These men had bled with him, trained under him, shared the weight of battles past.

"Do not be deceived by their numbers!" he thundered, his

voice carrying over the battlements. "They think they can crush us underfoot, like ants before their horde. They think us weak, but they do not know us. They do not understand what it means to fight for something greater than greed or ambition."

His words hung heavy in the air as he paused, his gaze sweeping over the gathered soldiers.

"But we" he continued, his voice growing fiercer, "we are the sons of Epiris! The shield that stands between the darkness and our homes. If they think we will falter, they are fools. If they think they will break us, they are wrong. Today, we will break them!"

A murmur rippled through the ranks, low but steady, growing louder as confidence began to take root. Apius raised his sword high, the blade catching the final rays of sunlight.

"We do not fight for glory or riches. We fight for our families, for our city, and for the land that is ours by blood and by right. Let them come! We will show them what it means to stand against Epiris!"

The first trebuchet stone crashed into the northern wall, shattering the moment of calm. Shards of stone rained down, and a plume of dust rose into the air. Apius didn't flinch. His voice rang out again, sharp and commanding.

"Archers, to your stations! Aim for the siege engines! Let none escape your mark!"

He turned to Captain Beran, a young officer whose face betrayed his inexperience despite his steady demeanour. "Reinforce the left flank. Keep them off the walls as long as you can."

"Yes, Your Majesty," Beran said, his voice tight with resolve.

Apius turned back toward the plains. The enemy's vanguard surged forward, ladders hoisted high as the first wave of soldiers charged the walls. A flood of bodies, he thought bitterly. This wasn't a battle of strategy—it was sheer, brute force.

"Loose!" he commanded, and the sky darkened with arrows. The first volley struck true, cutting into the enemy's ranks. Ladders toppled, men fell screaming to the ground, but the tide didn't stop. More ladders rose to take their place, and soon the walls were crawling with soldiers.

Apius drew his sword, its weight familiar in his hand. The battle would soon reach the walls, and he would not sit idly by while his city burned.

The first enemy soldier scrambled over the battlements, his sword raised. Apius stepped forward, slicing clean through the man's chest. Another followed, then another. Each fell to the King's blade as his bodyguard fought fiercely at his side.

"Hold the line!" Apius roared, his voice carrying over the chaos. Blood splattered across his armour as he struck down another attacker, his movements relentless despite the searing pain in his arm.

The walls trembled under the onslaught. Ladders rose like jagged shadows, and the enemy surged forward in greater numbers. Apius's men fought valiantly, cutting down attackers as they reached the top, but the tide was overwhelming. The meat grind wore on as time passed and the King had to cycle out to rest behind his guard.

A messenger sprinted toward him, breathless. "Your Majesty! The gates, they've breached the gates!"

Apius swore under his breath, his mind racing. The outer defences were crumbling. There was no time to hold the walls.

"Fall back!" he commanded, his voice cutting through the

din of battle. "All units to the inner gates! Regroup and hold the line there!"

His bodyguard pulled him away, their shields raised to block incoming blows. Reluctantly, Apius allowed himself to be led down the narrow stone steps, his sword still in hand. Behind him, the sound of battle raged on, growing fainter with each step.

The streets of Epiris were chaos. Smoke billowed into the sky as fires consumed the lower districts. Civilians screamed, fleeing deeper into the city as enemy soldiers poured through the gates. Apius's heart clenched at the sight.

They reached the inner gates, where a second line of defence had been hastily constructed. Soldiers scrambled to form ranks, their faces pale but determined. Apius, gripping his sword tightly as he turned to address his men.

"This is not over," he said, his voice low but steady. "We may have lost the outer walls, but Epiris still stands. And as long as we stand, this city will not fall."

As the enemy surged closer, Apius cast one final glance at the burning streets behind him. His jaw tightened, and his grip on his sword steadied.

This is not the end, he thought. Not yet.

Chapter 30

Spring 1308 Epiris City

As the trebuchets tore gaping holes in the once, imposing walls of Epiris, Widow surveyed the chaos before him with an air of triumph.

"So this is the mighty Epiris, stronghold of the King of Valhelm" he muttered, spreading his arms wide as if to embrace the morning sun. Smoke rose thick and black, smothering the horizon as ladders were hauled forward and slammed against the crumbling battlements.

Felix, now clad in a full set of mismatched armour scavenged from the eastern forests, turned to his new master. His brow furrowed as he watched the siege equipment batter the city's defences. "How do you plan on defeating the King's army? Their forces still stand strong" he asked sceptically, though he couldn't help but nod at the trebuchets' destructive progress.

"It's simple" Widow replied, his tone calm yet cutting as steel. "We cut the head off the snake."

The clang of steel echoed faintly from the walls as the first wave of attackers began to spill over the battlements.

Widow smiled faintly and barked his next command. "Fire. Raze it all to the ground."

A young messenger darted off, carrying the order to the trebuchet teams. Moments later, large clay pots filled with sticky black pitch were rolled into place. Torches were thrust into their contents, setting them ablaze with bright, licking flames.

The command came, and the siege crews unleashed their incendiary missiles. Clay pots smashed against the city walls and rooftops, the flaming pitch clinging to stone, wood, and flesh alike. Fire spread quickly, devouring everything it touched. Even the defenders' attempts to extinguish the flames only served to stoke the inferno.

"Use everything" Widow ordered, his voice calm despite the destruction he orchestrated. "I want it burnt to ash."

Turning back to Felix, Widow beckoned him to mount up. They both swung onto their horses, the noise of the battlefield around them a cacophony of chaos.

"I keep my word, Felix." Widow noted, his hawk like eyes surveying the scene.

Felix's gaze lingered on the flames and the defenders scrambling to plug the breaches in their city's walls. His doubts remained, but he kept them buried beneath a mask of stoic resolve.

The King's defenders, overwhelmed by the relentless assault, began to fall back toward the inner gates. Widow's lips curled into a satisfied grin. With a flick of the reins, he spurred his horse forward, leading his handpicked contingent of men down toward the base of the walls.

Widow had chosen his warriors carefully, the largest and most battle, hardened from among Rok's forces. They rode through acrid smoke, their horses snorting and pawing the ground nervously as the thick black haze stung their eyes. By the time they passed the outer wall and entered the city, the fighting had grown sporadic. Most of the resistance had retreated to the inner gates.

The wealthy district loomed ahead, a ring of grand townhouses and businesses reserved for the elite of Epiris. Beyond it rose the King's Hall, perched high on a rocky escarpment that overlooked the entire city. Widow reined in his horse and dismounted, his eyes fixed on the sheer rock face that led to the rear of the hall.

After dispatching Rok the previous night, Widow had searched his belongings and found a map detailing a hidden path, one that bypassed the heavily guarded gates. The first half of the climb was concealed by the wealthy district's towering buildings. Widow couldn't help but admire the plan. It was cunning, so cunning, in fact, that he'd decided to use it himself.

"We leave the horses here" Widow instructed, his tone sharp. "No sense in arousing suspicion."

The group of twenty men plus Felix dismounted, letting their horses loose into the courtyard. Widow's cold gaze lingered on the climb ahead. The cliff was jagged and steep, but it was their key to bypassing the King's defences.

Felix followed silently, gripping the hilt of his sword. He glanced at the other men, their brutish forms casting long shadows in the hazy light. They were killers, not climbers, and doubt gnawed at him. Would they even make it to the top? And if they did, would they still have the strength to fight?

Widow reached the rock face first, his movements deliberate and practised as he began the ascent. The loose gravel and sharp edges were no deterrent to him. "Keep up" he hissed over his shoulder. "And keep quiet. One slip, and I'll toss you down myself."

The men climbed in near silence, their breaths heavy with exertion. The sharp rock cut into their gloves and boots, and the occasional misstep sent small showers of stones tumbling downward. A younger soldier slipped, his foot skidding on a patch of moss. He froze, clinging to the rock, his breathing ragged.

Widow's voice cut through the tension like a whip. "Move, or I'll kill you myself before gravity does."

The soldier nodded shakily and resumed climbing.

The air grew colder as they ascended. Smoke from the burning city below stung their eyes, mixing with the acrid tang of sweat. Widow pressed on, his focus unyielding. The final stretch of the climb was the most treacherous. The rock face steepened, slick with moisture, but Widow scaled it with the ease of a predator stalking its prey.

When he reached the top, he crouched low, his sharp eyes scanning the surroundings. The rear of the King's Hall was just ahead, its imposing stone walls faintly illuminated by distant torchlight. One by one, the others joined him, their breaths laboured but their resolve intact.

"Move" Widow ordered. His voice was barely a whisper, but it carried the weight of command.

They advanced like shadows, slipping through the darkness with deadly purpose. Widow's men split into pairs, following his precise directions as they encircled the hall. Felix's grip on his sword tightened. The sound of battle echoed faintly from the lower city a grim reminder of the chaos Widow had unleashed.

When they reached the hall's outer wall, Widow turned to Felix, a wicked grin splitting his face. "This is where the fun begins."

Two guards stood outside the barred doors of the hall, their spears resting lazily at their sides. They were dead before they even realised they were under attack. Widow's men moved swiftly, dragging the bodies into the shadows and taking their positions around the entrance.

Felix stepped forward, his heart pounding as he rapped his gloved fist against the heavy oak door. His voice carried the perfect pitch of urgency and authority. "It's Felix! Captain of the Prince's army. The inner gates are breached, we need to move the King before we're cut off!"

After a tense pause, a viewing hatch slid open. A pair of eyes scrutinised Felix before the hatch slammed shut again. The sound of bolts being drawn back followed, and the door creaked open.

"Captain Felix! It's good to see you!" the guard exclaimed, beckoning him inside.

Felix forced a tight smile and stepped into the smaller entrance hall. He exchanged a few cordial words with the guard, his chest tightening with every step he took.

The next few moments would cement his betrayal. There was no turning back now.

Chapter 31

Spring 1308 Woodland overlooking Epiris City

Pesus ducked into the command tent, his eyes landing on Pax, who stood warming himself by the brazier in the corner, his back to the Grand Marshal.

"You made it back to us, then, Pax?"

When Pax turned, Pesus no longer saw the face of a boy. The ordeal had changed him, he had become a man.

"Yes, sir, thanks to Captain Ghoshte and his men."

Ghoshte shook his head, deflecting the credit, but Pesus strode forward, pulling Pax into a firm embrace.

"Well" Pesus said, stepping back and gripping the young man by the shoulders, "try to stick with us this time. I made a promise to your mother to bring you home safe, and I intend to keep it."

Pax's eyes lit up, a warmth flooding his chest.

Reading his thoughts, Pesus gave a reassuring nod. "Outside Juntya, I met your father too. They're both safe and very proud of you. I told them I'd bring you back."

Pax blinked rapidly, his emotions threatening to overwhelm him. He had never expected to see his parents again.

When Juntya fell, he had presumed them dead. This news filled him with hope he hadn't allowed himself to feel.

Ghoshte placed a reassuring hand on his shoulder, sensing the young man's turmoil.

The tent flap opened again, and Prince Althern stepped through, carrying a basket of bread, cheese, and salted meats. He set it down on the table with a clatter and eased into his seat, his movements deliberate and slow. The toll of recent battles was written in the exhaustion lining his face.

"Sit. Eat" Althern said, gesturing to the food. "You'll need your energy for this one."

As Althern laid out his plan, the men ate in contemplative silence, knowing this might be their last meal. Pax chewed his bread thoughtfully, wondering how his life had become a constant string of dangers.

The Prince's strategy was clear. He needed to warn his father of Felix's betrayal before it was too late. Althern would lead Pax and a small cavalry force through the breaches in the enemy lines to reach the King's Hall, where the King was surely still commanding the defence. Meanwhile, Pesus, Daka, Bones, and Ghoshte would lead their forces in a counterstrike, waiting for the enemy to breach the inner gates. When the moment was right, they would hit Widow's forces from behind, sowing chaos in the enemy ranks.

The sun had risen, casting a pale light over the forest. The distant sounds of battle carried faintly on the breeze as Althern mounted his horse and walked alongside Pax.

"Pesus tells me you've made a name for yourself in a sword fight" Althern said, a faint smile tugging at his lips.

Caught off guard by the compliment, Pax shrugged. "I've got a good sword in my hand. That's half the work."

Althern chuckled. "Modest, too. You've got skill, Pax. I won't let your talents go to waste."

The cavalry moved out of the forest's shelter, timing their advance for when most of the enemy had breached the city. The trebuchets had shifted their fire, targeting the upper levels of Epiris with devastating precision. Smoke billowed into the air as the defenders scrambled to regroup.

The Prince divided his cavalry. He placed fifteen men under Pax's command to target the outer trebuchets, while he led the rest against the siege engines closer to the city walls. Pax followed his orders, taking his group on a wide arc toward the tree line to avoid detection.

The pounding of hooves drummed in Pax's ears as they neared their first target. His heart raced, the wind biting at his face. They were within two hundred paces when Althern's group split, charging straight at the artillery crews. Pax mirrored the manoeuvre, taking his group wide to flank the furthest trebuchet.

"Form a wedge" Pax called over the thunder of hooves. "Don't stop to fight, just charge them down!"

The cavalry shifted smoothly into formation, their mounts snorting and stamping as they gathered speed.

"To Althern!" Pax roared, his voice carrying over the din.

The enemy crews, realising too late that they were unprotected, scrambled to defend themselves. Arrows flew, but most went wide in their panic. With no spears or reinforcements, the artillery teams began to scatter.

Pax's horse ploughed into a fleeing soldier, the sickening crunch of bones shattering beneath the hooves barely registering over the chaos. He gritted his teeth, setting his sights on the next trebuchet crew. An enemy archer loosed an arrow, the projectile striking Pax's chest plate with a loud clang but failing to pierce the steel.

Moments later, Pax's mount collided with the archer, the

sheer force throwing the man to the ground like a rag doll. The trebuchet crews lay in disarray, their machines silenced.

By the time Pax regrouped with Althern, all four trebuchets were destroyed, their crews either dead or fleeing. The Prince raised his sword in triumph, his men cheering as the tide shifted in their favour.

Allowing the horses a moment's rest, Althern and Pax led the group through the remnants of the enemy camp. Fires smouldered in abandoned pits, and scattered supplies lay forgotten in the dirt. As they passed the tent where Widow had murdered Rok, Pax's stomach churned. He chose to say nothing, knowing it would only add to Althern's burden.

They approached the city walls cautiously, their mounts treading over the bodies of fallen soldiers. The crows were already gathering, their harsh cries filling the air. A breach in the wall, created by a massive boulder from the trebuchets, provided their entry point.

The rhythmic pounding of a battering ram shook the ground as the group advanced through the gap. The enemy was attempting to break through the west gate, a smaller entrance leading to the inner city.

"Stick close" Althern ordered, his voice low. "The shortest route is through this side, but the gate's under attack. We'll need to find a way through."

"How many men at the gate?" Pax asked, scanning the narrow street.

"About a hundred," Althern replied grimly. "Hopefully, most are at the main inner gate."

As they neared the final street, Althern dismounted. Handing his reins to Pax, he drew his sword.

"Stay here. Keep the horses quiet" he commanded.

"What if you get captured?" Pax protested, gripping the reins tightly.

Althern smiled faintly. "You've already been captured on my behalf once, Pax. I'll be fine."

He disappeared around the corner, leaving the group in tense silence. Minutes dragged by, each one heavier than the last. The men shifted nervously, their eyes darting to every shadow.

When Althern finally returned, his expression was grim.

"They're nearly through. About a hundred men. When they breach, that's our moment to strike."

He turned to Pax and handed him the Prince's banner. "You'll hold this in the centre. Keep it high. If it falls, this will fail. Someone at the inner gate must see it."

Pax nodded, gripping the banner tightly. The group edged forward, positioning themselves at the corner of the street. The crack of splintering wood echoed through the air.

"They're in" Althern said. "Now. Let's go!"

The cavalry surged forward, their formation tightening into a deadly wedge. Pax rode at the centre, the banner held aloft as the gap between them and the enemy disappeared.

The attackers, still focused on breaking through the second gate, didn't notice the cavalry until it was too late. Althern's men crashed into the rear of the enemy lines, cutting through with brutal efficiency.

From above, defenders unleashed burning oil and pitch, followed by volleys of arrows. The attackers, trapped between the cavalry and the flames, descended into chaos.

Pax waved the banner frantically, praying for the defenders to notice. As arrows rained down on the enemy, the gate creaked open, and Althern's group charged through.

The moment they cleared the gate, it slammed shut behind them, cutting off pursuit. Althern's horse, its legs scorched by the oil, bucked wildly, throwing the Prince to the ground.

"Water for the horses!" Althern shouted. "Wash their legs!"

The men worked quickly, dousing the animals with buckets of water. Althern, brushing himself off, turned to his soldiers.

"These horses have done enough. We go the rest of the way on foot."

Twenty men remained, two too injured to continue. Leaving them to tend the horses, Althern led the rest down the narrow street toward the King's Hall.

As they approached the towering structure, its stone walls glowing faintly in the morning light, one thought weighed heavily on Althern's mind.

Was it already too late?

CHAPTER 32

SPRING 1308 INNER EPIRIS CITY

The streets of Epiris were choked with smoke and filled with the cries of the dying. Embers from nearby fires cast flickering shadows across blood soaked cobblestones. The enemy had spread through much of the city, their forces flooding avenues and twisting alleys in a chaotic sprawl of steel and death. Yet, Grand Marshal Pesus saw not chaos, it was a battlefield primed for strategy.

Standing at the forefront of his men, Pesus surveyed the scene with sharp, calculating eyes. Behind him, Captain Daka and Captain Bones waited for orders, their detachments ready to move. From a rooftop overlooking the central square, Captain Ghoshte and his archers lay poised, their arrows ready to rain destruction on the enemy.

Pesus turned to his captains, his voice steady but laden with authority. "Daka, drive them down the western street and cut off their retreat. Bones, press the eastern flank. Compact them. We'll funnel them into the square." He pointed toward the narrowest section of the central avenue. "Ghoshte, hold your fire until they're boxed in. Once they have nowhere to go, let the arrows do their work."

Daka gave a sharp nod, his face resolute. "We'll drive them like cattle, Marshal. Count on it."

Bones smirked, the scars on his face illuminated by the glow of nearby flames. "And once they're packed tight, we'll bleed them dry."

Pesus's gaze hardened. "No mistakes. Keep the formations tight. This is our city, and we will not lose it."

Captain Daka stepped forward, his men forming up behind him in disciplined ranks. The shield wall advanced down the western street with precision, the sound of boots hammering cobblestones in unison echoing through the narrowing passage.

The enemy forces ahead noticed the movement, quickly forming a ragged line of spearmen to meet the advancing shield wall. Daka raised his sword high, his voice commanding.

"Shields up! Brace for impact!"

The spearmen charged, their shouts ringing through the tight confines of the street, but Daka's men held firm. Shields locked together, they absorbed the first wave. The clash of steel against wood echoed as enemy spears splintered against their defences.

"Push!" Daka roared. The shield wall surged forward, driving the enemy back step by step. The soldiers thrust their spears with deadly precision, cutting through the front ranks of the attackers.

The enemy faltered, their formation crumbling as panic set in. Daka allowed himself a grim smile. "They're breaking. Drive them to the square!"

On the eastern side, Captain Bones was already advancing. His light infantry swept through the narrow alleys, cutting off escape routes with ruthless efficiency. Bones led the charge himself, his massive two handed sword cleaving through enemy shields and armour as if they were parchment.

"Keep moving!" Bones bellowed, his voice like thunder. "Don't let up until they've got nowhere left to run!"

Daka's men pressed from the west as Bones's forces closed in from the east. The enemy soldiers were driven into the central avenue, their ranks forced tighter and tighter with every step.

Above, perched on the rooftops, Captain Ghoshte crouched low, his keen eyes scanning the chaos below. Beside him knelt Casius, his bow drawn and his young face illuminated by the firelight. Ghoshte had trained him for weeks, sharpening the boy's raw talent into something deadly. Tonight, that training would be tested.

"They're bunching up" Ghoshte murmured, his voice calm and deliberate. "Not yet. Let them panic first. Desperation makes them clumsy."

Casius nodded, though his stomach churned with nerves. He had hunted wild boars and deer in the forests, but these weren't animals. These were men, armed and brutal. His fingers flexed on the bowstring, instinct urging him to fire, but Ghoshte's measured presence beside him steadied his hand.

On the ground below, the enemy's situation grew more chaotic by the moment. Daka and Bones's coordinated assault had driven them into the square, their ranks packed together like cattle awaiting slaughter. Ghoshte raised his hand, his sharp gaze following the movement of the enemy forces as the final pieces of the trap fell into place.

"Casius" Ghoshte said, his voice steady as stone. "This is where the real hunt begins. Remember: breathe, aim, loose. No hesitation. These men will show you no mercy, so give them none in return."

Casius nodded once more, his hands steadying as he drew the bowstring back. Ghoshte's words echoed in his mind, sharpening his focus.

The signal came, a sharp flare of light from the eastern flank. Ghoshte's hand dropped.

"Loose!"

A volley of arrows streaked through the night, their fletching catching the faint light of the fires. The first wave struck with brutal accuracy, cutting through the enemy ranks in the centre of the square. Screams pierced the air as bodies crumpled to the ground, panic spreading like wildfire.

Casius released his first arrow. It flew straight and true, striking a soldier in the shoulder and spinning him around before he collapsed. There was no time to think about the kill. His hands moved instinctively, nocking another arrow, drawing, loosing.

"Good" Ghoshte muttered, loosing an arrow of his own into the crowd below. "Keep the rhythm. Aim for the gaps in their armour. Take out the officers first."

Casius adjusted his aim, spotting a man barking orders in the centre of the chaos. His arrow struck the officer's thigh, dropping him to his knees. Moments later, another archer's shot finished him off.

The enemy's panic was palpable now, their cohesion shattered as more volleys rained down. Soldiers attempted to raise shields, but the packed formation left them little room to manoeuvre. Others tried to flee, only to be cut down by Daka and Bones's advancing forces.

"Casius, there!" Ghoshte snapped, pointing to a group of soldiers attempting to regroup near the southern edge of the square.

Casius shifted his aim, his movements fluid now, each shot landing with deadly precision. The whitehot nerves that had gripped him earlier were gone, replaced by a cold, focused determination.

But then he saw him, a young enemy soldier scrambling for cover, his face pale with terror. The boy couldn't have been much older than Casius himself. For a moment, Casius hesitated, his breath catching in his throat.

"Do it" Ghoshte barked. "Hesitation gets you killed. You won't save anyone if they overrun the city."

Casius exhaled slowly, releasing the arrow. It struck the boy cleanly in the chest. He fell, motionless. Casius's stomach churned, but he forced himself to nock another arrow. The twisting in his chest hardened into resolve.

On the ground, Pesus watched as the plan unfolded perfectly. The enemy, disorganised and leaderless, were compressed into the square, driven like livestock to slaughter. Daka and Bones's coordinated assault crushed any remaining resistance, while Ghoshte's archers picked off stragglers with ruthless efficiency.

Pesus's lips curled into a faint smile. This is how you win a war.

He raised his sword, its blade gleaming in the firelight. "Advance! Wipe them out!"

The defenders surged forward, shields raised and swords gleaming. Pesus strode into the fray, his presence a steadying force for his men. His blade flashed, cutting down one enemy soldier, then another, his movements deliberate and precise.

Within minutes, the enemy's rear forces had been annihilated. The central square lay still, littered with the bodies of the fallen. Pesus stepped forward, surveying the battlefield with a critical eye.

"Captain Daka" he said, his tone measured, "secure the square. No stragglers."

Daka saluted crisply. "Yes, Marshal."

"Bones" Pesus continued, "take your men and sweep the eastern streets. The city's not safe yet."

Bones nodded grimly. "On it."

As his captains moved to carry out their orders, Pesus sheathed his sword. The moans of the wounded and the crackling of distant fires filled the air. They had bought the city a sliver of hope, but the battle was far from over.

Pesus turned his gaze toward the distant silhouette of the King's Hall, its towering walls faintly lit by the glow of the fires. This is only the beginning, he thought grimly. The real fight is yet to come.

Chapter 33

Spring 1308 Kings Hall Epiris City

The front of the King's Hall was eerily silent, save for the faint crackle of distant fires licking at the edges of the city. Pax's heart pounded against his ribs as he followed Althern and the eighteen cavalry soldiers along the stone path leading to the towering doors. His palms were slick on the hilt of the sword Althern had given him, the weight of his father's craftsmanship feeling heavier than ever.

As they approached, something caught Pax's eye, a body slumped near the grand archway. The flickering torchlight cast long shadows over its lifeless form, and Pax's stomach churned.

"Here" Pax hissed, kneeling beside the corpse. The sight sent a wave of nausea through him. A palace guard, his throat cut cleanly, blood pooling beneath him in a dark halo.

Althern crouched beside him, his jaw tightening as he studied the wound. "Felix" he muttered, his voice thick with anger and disbelief. "This was his blade."

Pax's eyes widened. "How can you be sure?"

Althern pointed to the distinctive curve of the gash. "Felix was cavalry before he became my Captain. He was trained for precision, to kill quickly and cleanly. This" Althern's voice faltered, a mix of fury and grief. "this is his work."

Before Pax could respond, a muffled crash echoed from within the hall. The sound of a struggle. Raised voices, harsh and angry. Then something heavy toppled to the floor.

"Inside!" Althern barked, drawing his sword and charging toward the doors. His men followed without hesitation, Pax gripping his blade tightly as he ran to keep up.

The sight that greeted them inside the hall made Pax's breath catch in his throat.

The grand chamber—once a place of power and elegance, was a vision of chaos. The King's personal guard lay dead across the polished stone floor, their bodies strewn like broken dolls. Blood smeared the walls and pooled beneath overturned chairs. The long dining table had been shattered into jagged splinters.

In the centre of it all knelt King Apius, his once, pristine armour smeared with blood and dirt. His shoulders sagged under the weight of defeat, but his eyes still burned with defiance. Behind him stood Felix, one arm wrapped around the King's shoulders, the other pressing a blade against his throat.

The King's gaze flicked upward as Althern burst into the hall. His expression, a heart-wrenching mix of defiance, sorrow, and a father's love, seemed to pierce through Althern's armour.

Across the room, Widow leaned against a stone column, his jewelled sword dangling lazily from his fingers. Around him, twenty of his men stood tense and ready, their weapons gleaming in the dim torchlight. Widow's lips curled into a sly grin as he spotted Althern.

"Well, well," Widow drawled, his voice thick with mockery. "If it isn't the prodigal son, come to save the day."

Althern's grip on his sword tightened, his knuckles

whitening. His voice trembled with rage, though he forced it to remain steady. "Release him, Widow. This isn't a game."

Widow chuckled, a low, sinister sound that reverberated through the blood-soaked hall. "A game? Oh no, Prince. This is history in the making. Tonight, I end a broken dynasty. When the bards sing of this moment, they'll tell the tale of how I razed Epiris and built a kingdom from its ashes. I'll build a better kingdom than your father ever has. Stronger. More developed. Unshackled by weakness."

"Let him go," Althern said, his voice now firmer, colder. "You can still leave here alive."

Widow's grin widened. "Leave here alive? Oh, how quaint, you've already been saved once by your boy. Pathetic, you'll kneel before me, or join your father in the dirt."

The words hung heavy in the air, but Althern didn't falter. "You're deluded, Widow."

Widow took a step forward, his head tilting as if studying Althern. "Deluded? No. But I've always wondered something." His voice turned venomous. "What's it like, Althern? Carrying that desperate, pathetic look everywhere you go. The one that says, 'Why wasn't I ever good enough for him?'"

Althern froze.

Widow's smirk deepened as he continued, his tone biting. "You weren't his favourite, were you? That was Rok. Poor, perfect Rok. You? You were just the spare. The soldier boy playing at being a Prince. You're not angry because I'm killing him. You're angry because you'll never hear him say he was proud of you."

The words sliced through Althern, each syllable sharper than a blade. Widow knew the exact wound to twist, and he relished it. Althern's sword arm wavered for a fraction of a second, his rage tempered by old wounds Widow had torn open.

But then, from the corner of the room, King Apius lifted his head. His lips moved silently, but Althern saw the words clearly:

"You are enough, my son."

Tears pricked Althern's eyes, but the moment was shattered as Widow turned sharply. "Felix" he snapped, his voice cold as steel. "Do it. Now."

Felix's blade pressed harder, and with a swift, merciless motion, he dragged the knife across King Apius's throat. The King's eyes widened in shock as blood poured from the wound, streaking his chest. He slumped forward, lifeless.

"No!" Althern's scream tore through the hall as he surged forward, his blade flashing.

His sword met Felix's with a furious clash of sparks and steel. "You traitor!" Althern roared, his strikes coming hard and fast. "You killed him!"

Felix parried, his movements precise and unyielding. "He was weak" Felix snarled, meeting Althern's fury with cold precision. "Just like you."

The clang of steel on steel echoed through the hall as they fought. Widow, meanwhile, slipped toward the doorway, cutting down one of Althern's men with a savage swing.

"Widow!" Althern shouted, his voice raw and desperate.

Widow glanced back, his grin sharp and mocking. "Sorry, Prince. I have a kingdom to claim." And with that, he vanished into the chaos beyond.

Althern hesitated, his focus divided, and Felix seized the moment. He drove his shoulder into Althern's chest, sending him sprawling to the bloodied floor.

Felix raised his sword, ready to deliver the killing blow.

But before he could strike, Pax lunged forward, his father's blade gleaming as it intercepted the strike.

"Stay away from him!" Pax shouted, his voice trembling with fear and determination.

Felix staggered, his expression darkening in frustration. Althern rolled to his feet, his blade cutting upward in a desperate arc. The force knocked Felix's sword from his hand, sending it clattering to the floor.

Disarmed and outnumbered, Felix glared at Althern one last time before turning and bolting for the door.

"Felix!" Althern shouted, but the traitor was gone, vanishing into the shadows after Widow.

Althern turned to where his father's body lay. His knees buckled, and he collapsed beside him. Blood seeped through the King's armour, pooling around him in a dark stain that seemed to extinguish the light from the torches.

"I'm sorry" Althern whispered, his voice broken. "I should've been faster. I should've—" His words choked off as tears spilled down his face.

King Apius, the man who had held a kingdom together with strength and resolve, was gone.

Around him, the hall fell into an eerie silence. The battle had ended, but its cost was immeasurable.

Chapter 34

Spring 1308 Epiris City

The streets of Epiris lay shrouded in an eerie quiet, broken only by the faint crackle of fires devouring what remained of the city. Smoke hung heavy in the air, curling like ghostly fingers around the rubble of once proud buildings. Captain Bones led his men cautiously through the shadowed alleys, their armour clinking and boots crunching over debris. The battle was all but won, but danger still lingered, scattered remnants of the enemy lurked in the ruins, scavenging, hiding, or waiting for a chance to strike.

Bones paused at the corner of a collapsed bakery, his broad shoulders heaving as he caught his breath. His massive two-handed sword rested against his shoulder, the blade crusted with blood and soot.

"Eyes sharp," he growled, his voice low and gravelly. "If they're still breathing, they're still a threat."

His soldiers nodded, spreading out in pairs to search the surrounding buildings. Bones lingered, his instincts gnawing at him. Something about the silence wasn't right. It wasn't the quiet of peace, it was the quiet of something lying in wait.

A flicker of movement caught his eye. He stiffened. At

the far end of the street, a shadow slipped into the cover of an alleyway, quick and deliberate.

"You there!" Bones bellowed, his voice echoing through the empty streets. "Come out where I can see you!"

There was no answer. Only the faint rustle of disturbed debris.

He took a step forward, his eyes narrowing as they searched the darkness. Slowly, a figure emerged from the shadows, striding into the dim torchlight with a lazy, predatory swagger.

Widow.

The bandit leader smiled, a dangerous curve of his lips that didn't reach his cold, calculating eyes. His sword dangled loosely from his hand, its polished edge gleaming faintly in the firelight.

"Well, if it isn't the walking buffoon" Widow drawled, his tone mocking. "Captain Bones, wasn't it? You've been busy, haven't you? Cutting through my men like a butcher in a slaughterhouse."

Bones squared his shoulders, his towering frame casting a long shadow across the rubble strewn street. "Widow" he said, his voice low and menacing. "You're not leaving this city alive."

Widow's grin widened. "Big words from a man who's bleeding from half a dozen cuts. Swinging that oversized blade all night must've taken it out of you."

Bones's jaw clenched, his grip tightening on his sword. He began to step forward, but froze as something flickered in his peripheral vision. High above, a pale figure moved silently along the rooftops, the white wolf. Its golden eyes shone like twin lanterns in the dark, fixed intently on him.

For a brief moment, the world seemed to still. Bones felt a strange chill run through him, and yet, there was a quiet certainty in his chest. This is it, he thought. This is where it ends.

With a guttural roar, Bones surged forward, his massive blade raised high. Widow laughed, sidestepping the initial swing with practiced ease. The bandit's curved sword snapped up in a quick counterstrike, but Bones deflected it with a flick of his wrist.

The clash of steel rang out, sharp and deafening, as the narrow street erupted into chaos. Widow's soldiers spilled from the alleyways, their weapons flashing in the dim light. Bones's men met them with brutal force, the small street becoming a whirlwind of violence. But Bones hardly noticed. His entire focus was locked on Widow.

Widow was fast far faster than Bones had anticipated. He moved like smoke, darting and weaving around Bones's heavy strikes, his polished blade flickering dangerously close with every pass. But Bones was no novice. Each swing of his greatsword was precise, calculated, and devastating, forcing Widow to give ground with every attack.

"Is this it?" Widow taunted, breathless but still grinning. "All that size, all that fury and still too slow."

Bones ignored him, his strikes growing more relentless. Widow's grin began to falter as he struggled to keep up, his movements losing their confident fluidity. Around them, the fight raged on. One by one, Bones's men cut down the last of Widow's soldiers, until only their leader remained standing.

From the edge of the alley, Ghoshte and Casius arrived, their weapons drawn and their eyes darting between the remaining combatants.

"Bones!" Ghoshte shouted, his voice sharp with concern. "Do you need help?"

Bones didn't look back. "Stay out of this!" he barked, his voice a thunderclap in the chaos. "This one's mine!"

Ghoshte hesitated, his hand twitching on his bow. But he knew better than to disobey his fellow Captain. He stepped back, his sharp gaze scanning the alley for other threats.

Casius lingered, torn between stepping in and respecting Bones's command. His eyes flicked to the rooftops, where the white wolf had disappeared moments earlier. Without a word, he turned and began climbing, his bow slung over his shoulder, determination etched into his young face.

Meanwhile, the duel raged on. Bones's strength was undeniable, his greatsword carving through the air in wide, punishing arcs. Widow dodged and deflected, but each parry left his arm trembling under the force of Bones's strikes.

"You're slipping" Widow sneered, feinting to one side before darting in with a quick slash. His blade sliced across Bones's thigh, cutting through armour and flesh.

Bones staggered, pain flaring in his leg. Blood seeped down to his boot, but he didn't fall. He gritted his teeth, raising his sword once more.

Widow laughed, circling him like a vulture. "That's it, big man. Bleed for me. Bleed and die."

Bones roared again, swinging his sword in a desperate arc. Widow leapt back, narrowly avoiding the blade's edge. But Bones's movements were slowing. His wounds were beginning to take their toll.

Widow saw his chance. He darted in, his strikes coming faster now, more precise. His blade scored a shallow cut across Bones's arm, then another along his ribs.

Above them, Casius crouched on the rooftop, his bow drawn. He watched the fight below with grim focus, his breathing steady. Widow raised his sword for the killing blow, his grin widening as he moved to strike.

Casius loosed the arrow.

The shot was perfect. The arrow struck Widow in the

chest, the force of the impact staggering him. His blade faltered, falling from his grasp as he collapsed to his knees, blood soaking the front of his tunic.

Bones stared, disbelief flickering across his face. Then he turned, his eyes finding the figure on the rooftop. Casius stood silhouetted against the smoke-filled sky, his bow still in hand.

A faint smile tugged at the corner of Bones's mouth as he saw the fletching of the arrow punctuating Widows chest. "Casius" he murmured, his voice barely audible.

Widow collapsed forward, his body hitting the bloodied cobblestones with a lifeless thud. The street fell silent, save for the heavy breathing of Bones and his men.

From the next street over, the sound of approaching hooves cut through the quiet. Grand Marshal Pesus rode into view, his destrier's flanks slick with sweat, his armour battered but still gleaming. His men followed close behind, their weapons drawn and their expressions grim.

Pesus dismounted in a fluid motion, striding toward Bones. His sharp eyes took in the scene, the dead soldiers, the blood-streaked cobblestones, and Widow's lifeless body.

"Bones" Pesus said, his tone even but edged with concern. "You're hurt."

Bones nodded, wiping blood from his face. "I'll live" he said, though his voice was hoarse. "It's over. Widow's dead."

Pesus's gaze shifted to the rooftops, where Casius was climbing down. "That shot" Pesus murmured, a note of approval in his voice. "Was it the boy?"

Bones nodded again, a faint smile breaking through his exhaustion. "He's got the makings of a damn fine soldier."

Pesus's lips pressed into a thin line. "We'll need him. This fight isn't over yet."

The Grand Marshal turned, his gaze fixed on the smouldering ruins of the city. Epiris was scarred, its streets littered with the dead, but the battle for the kingdom's future was only beginning.

"Regroup the men" Pesus ordered, his voice ringing with authority. "We march to the King's Hall."

And with that, the battered remnants of Epiris's defenders began their march, their hearts heavy but their resolve unbroken.

Chapter 35

Spring 1308 Epiris City

The King's Hall, once soaked in blood and grief, now bore the marks of restoration. The shattered furniture had been replaced, the bloodstains scrubbed painstakingly from the polished stone floors, and the banners of Epiris once more hung proudly from the high, vaulted walls. Yet no amount of cleaning could erase the weight of memory that lingered here, the loss of King Apius, the scars of the recent battle, and the burdens of a kingdom on the brink of rebuilding.

Althern sat at the head of the long dining table, his expression a careful balance of strength and weariness. Around him were the faces of those who had stood by him through every harrowing moment. To his left sat Pesus, the Grand Marshal, solid and unyielding as always. To his right, Ghoshte lounged slightly back, his piercing eyes roaming the room, assessing every detail. The chair meant for Captain Bones remained conspicuously empty, the man still recuperating under the watchful eye of a very vocal healer.

Daka sat further down the table, his quiet presence steadying. And Pax, young, yet brave beyond his years, had been invited to join them. His presence was a silent testament to the sacrifices made and the battles won, a reminder that the cost of war had been paid by men both seasoned and young.

The table was laden with an abundance of food: golden-roasted meats, freshly baked bread, bowls brimming with steamed vegetables. Goblets of wine and pitchers of ale were scattered across the surface, untouched for now.

Althern raised his goblet, his voice breaking the silence that hung over the room. "To all of you, my most loyal friends. You have given me your trust, your swords, and your very lives. For that, I will never stop being grateful."

A murmur of agreement passed through the group. Pesus inclined his head. "You have our loyalty, Your Grace. Always."

Setting his goblet down, Althern's tone grew more sombre. "The coronation will be held at the end of the week. The city needs time to stabilise, and the people must know that their king is here for them."

Pesus nodded, his gaze thoughtful. "A wise decision. Let them rebuild, let them see their leader walk among them. By the time the crown rests on your head, they'll rally behind you."

Ghoshte leaned forward, his arms resting on the table. "And what of Felix?" His voice was measured, though his tone betrayed a hint of unease. "The men are talking. They don't understand why he betrayed us, or how we didn't see it coming."

At the mention of Felix, a shadow fell across the room. Althern's jaw tightened, but he forced himself to answer. "I've thought about it endlessly. Felix was one of our best. I trusted him completely. My father did too."

Pesus frowned deeply, his expression darkening. "Did you know he came from the Ghober Wood?"

Althern's head snapped towards him, confusion flickering across his face. "No" he said slowly. "I didn't."

Pesus exhaled heavily, leaning forward as he explained. "Ghober wood lies in the heart of Rok and Widow's territory. If Felix was born there... perhaps they offered him something we couldn't. Or maybe his loyalty was never ours to begin with."

A bitter silence settled over the table, the weight of those words pressing down on everyone.

The tension was broken by the sudden burst of the hall doors. Captain Bones limped into the room, his broad frame wrapped in bandages, a disgruntled healer trailing behind him. Despite his obvious injuries, Bones's swagger remained intact.

"You started without me?" Bones grumbled, his gravelly voice laced with mock indignation. "Cruel, that is. Absolutely cruel." Helping prop up the giant of a man was Casius, clearly recruited by the bashful captain to help him escape the healers.

The healer glared at him, her small frame somehow brimming with authority. "Captain, you're supposed to be resting! You can't keep ignoring my orders!"

Bones waved her off with a grin, lowering himself into his chair with a wince. "I'll rest when I'm dead. Right now, there's chicken, and I'm not about to let it go cold." He tore a chunk of meat from a roasted drumstick with his teeth, chewing with exaggerated satisfaction.

The room erupted in laughter, the camaraderie breaking through the sombre atmosphere like sunlight through storm clouds. Even the healer let out an exasperated chuckle. Althern grinned, gesturing for her to leave him be. "He's your problem later, healer. For now, let him eat."

As the group settled into their meal, the laughter subsided, and Pesus leaned forward, his tone turning serious. "Your Grace, what will we do about Felix? He's still out there, and we can't ignore the danger he poses."

Althern nodded, setting down his goblet as his gaze turned inward. "Before my father…" His voice faltered momentarily, but he pressed on. "Before he was killed, he sent a runner to King Volneer beyond the Blackridge Mountains. If Felix or any remnants of Rok's forces have moved into those lands, Volneer will know. We should have word soon."

Pesus grunted in approval. "And if he's not there?"

"Then we'll find him ourselves" Althern said, his voice firm and resolute.

The conversation shifted. Althern's expression softened, and his tone grew contemplative. "I've been thinking about all of you. About what you've done for me, for the realm. None of this would have been possible without your courage, your sacrifices."

He turned to Pesus first. "Grand Marshal, I'll need you by my side. Your wisdom and strength will be more important than ever in the days to come."

Pesus smiled, a rare and genuine expression. "You'll have me, Your Grace, for as long as I draw breath."

Althern inclined his head before addressing Ghoshte and Bones. "And you two? Will you continue to serve as captains in my army?"

Ghoshte nodded. "You'll have my bow for as long as you need it."

Bones grinned through a mouthful of chicken. "You're stuck with me, lad. Try to get rid of me, and I'll just come back."

The room chuckled, and Althern's gaze shifted to Daka,

seated quietly near the centre of the table. "And you, Captain Daka? Will you stay?"

Daka smiled, shaking his head. "Your Grace, I've fought my battles. It's a younger man's game now. But if you'll have me, I'd like to stay in Epiris, training recruits, building the next generation of soldiers for the realm."

Althern's smile widened. "It would be an honour, Captain."

As the feast continued, Pesus spoke again, this time directing the conversation towards Pax. "Your Grace, if I may, Pax has proven himself beyond question. The men respect him, they've seen his bravery and his skill. I believe he could lead the cavalry as a captain, at least for now."

Althern raised an eyebrow, glancing at the young man. Pax shifted uncomfortably, his face flushing with surprise.

"You think he's ready?" Althern asked, his tone laced with playful doubt.

Pesus chuckled. "He has much to learn, but the potential is there. With guidance, he'll rise to the occasion."

Althern leaned back in his chair, smiling. "Then it's settled. Captain Pax, it seems you have your first command."

Pax blinked, his grip tightening on the goblet before managing a quiet nod. "Thank you, Your Grace. I won't let you down."

The evening wore on, the conversation turning to plans for rebuilding the city and strengthening the army. Althern spoke of the challenges ahead with determination, though the weight of responsibility was evident in his voice.

Bones finished his meal and emptied his tankard with a hearty belch. Casius was close at hand, ready to help him back to his chamber in the healer's wing. Rising stiffly from the table, Bones paused as a thought struck him. His hand drifted to his breast pocket, fingers fumbling with the button as he reached inside, searching for something.

Casius watched him curiously, his brow furrowed.

After a moment, Bones pulled out a silver necklace coiled neatly in his palm. He held it up, revealing a round white stone at its centre.

Casius gasped, his breath hitching. It was his mother's necklace.

"Casius" Bones began, his voice unusually soft, "I'm sorry. I'd forgotten about it until now. If I told you a white wolf asked me to give it to you, you'd probably think it was the wine talking. But that's exactly what happened."

Casius took the necklace carefully, his hands trembling as he held the familiar piece of jewellery. A tearful smile crossed his face.

"Amahra…" he murmured, clutching the necklace tightly. "Thank you for keeping this safe for me, Bones."

Without another word, he turned and walked out of the hall, the doors creaking softly as they swung shut behind him. Holding the necklace close to his heart, Casius disappeared into the corridor, leaving the Captain stranded at the table.

Bones didn't mind. If anything, it gave him an excuse to stay for another drink.

As the others talked and laughed, Althern grew quieter. His gaze drifted to the banners hanging from the walls, the vibrant colours catching the flickering torchlight. Memories of his father washed over him, their conversations, their disagreements, and the final moments they'd shared.

"You are enough" Apius had mouthed before his death.

Althern closed his eyes, holding onto that memory. The kingdom had been broken, but together, they would rebuild it.

And this time, it would stand stronger than ever.

Chapter 36

Spring 1308 Epiris City

The city of Epiris stirred under the gentle glow of dawn, its streets unusually calm after the chaos of recent days. Smoke from extinguished fires still lingered faintly in the air, curling around the edges of rooftops as the first rays of sunlight painted the cobblestones golden. Today, a weary but resilient kingdom prepared to crown Prince Althern as King a moment that would symbolise both the end of war and the beginning of uncertain peace.

But instead of donning robes or presiding over last minute preparations in the King's Hall, Althern was walking the familiar path to the cavalry stables. His boots crunched softly against the dirt road as he passed a handful of early risers setting up market stalls. They bowed deeply as he approached, their expressions a mixture of reverence and relief. Althern gave them a faint nod, his thoughts clearly elsewhere.

The scent of hay and leather greeted him as he entered the stables, the rhythmic shuffle of horses and the occasional snort breaking the silence. A group of stable boys, busy tending to the animals, froze when they saw him. Their faces turned pale, and they scrambled to bow clumsily.

"Your Grace!" one of them stammered, his voice high with panic. "You—you shouldn't be here. Let us—"

Althern raised a hand, cutting him off with a gentle smile. "Relax. I didn't come to give orders." He moved past them, his long strides carrying him to the far end of the stable row. There, in a stall apart from the others, stood a dark bay mustang. Shadow.

The horse had carried him through fire and battle, its endurance and courage saving them both more times than Althern could count. The faint scars on Shadow's legs, evidence of the burns he'd suffered during the siege, were healing well, though they would forever mark him as a survivor.

Shadow snorted softly as Althern opened the stall door and stepped inside. "Good boy" Althern murmured, his voice low and soothing as he stroked the horse's neck. He reached into a small wooden box at the back of the stall and pulled out a jar of salve. With practised care, he crouched and began applying the ointment to Shadow's legs. The horse shifted slightly, but Althern's steady hand and calming words kept him still.

From behind, the stable boys exchanged bewildered looks. Finally, one of them found the courage to speak. "Your Grace... it's not proper for a king to do that" he said hesitantly.

Althern chuckled softly, not bothering to look up from his task. "A king serves his people" he said simply. "And these horses are no less deserving of respect. They fought as hard as any man defending this city. They earned this care."

The boy blinked, unsure how to respond, and eventually fell silent.

By the time Althern finished tending to Shadow, footsteps echoed faintly down the stable corridor. He straightened, turning to see Pax approaching. The young man hesitated at the entrance, his posture uncertain as he surveyed the unexpected scene.

"Your Grace" Pax said, bowing awkwardly. "You sent for me?"

"I did" Althern replied, wiping his hands on a cloth before stepping out of the stall. "Come here."

Pax moved closer, glancing curiously at the horses lining the stalls. "Why meet here?" he asked.

Althern gestured toward the animals. "Eighteen of these horses survived the fires and the battle. They carried us through the hardest days this city has ever seen. I intend to honour them."

Pax furrowed his brow. "Honour them, Your Grace?"

Althern nodded, his expression softening. "I've decided to retire them. They'll be released to roam freely on the grounds where Rok's camp once stood. That land will now belong to them, under the protection of the crown."

Pax's gaze lingered on Shadow. "Even him?" he asked quietly.

Althern smiled faintly, shaking his head. "Not Shadow. I have a special task for him." He stepped over to a small table near the stable entrance, where two scrolls sat sealed with red wax. Picking them up, he turned back to Pax and held them out.

"These are for you," Althern said.

Pax took the scrolls carefully, his brow furrowing. "What are they?"

"The first," Althern explained, "is for your parents. You'll take Shadow and pull a small cart. Find them in Juntya and deliver this letter. Do not open it under any circumstances."

Pax clutched the scroll tightly, a flicker of emotion crossing his face. "And the second?"

"The second" Althern continued, his tone gentler now, "is for Marya. On your way back, you'll stop at her cabin and deliver it to her personally."

Pax's eyes widened slightly, but he nodded without question.

Althern placed a firm hand on the young man's shoulder. "Pax, you've proven yourself. To me, to the men, and to this kingdom. Pesus and the other captains agree, you will do well with your command."

Pax nodded his expression sincere "I just don't want to let anyone down?" his voice barely above a whisper.

"I know, learn from Pesus and the others, you will be okay." Althern confirmed, his smile growing. "Your first task is to rebuild the cavalry. Oversee the stables, secure new horses, and ensure they're trained well. The responsibility is yours."

Pax's cheeks flushed with pride and nerves, and he straightened, his grip on the scrolls tightening. "I won't let you down, Your Grace."

"I know you won't," Althern replied. "Now prepare Shadow and gather a small escort. Find your parents, deliver the scrolls, and return to Epiris within the week."

Pax bowed deeply before hurrying out of the stables, his steps carrying an air of purpose and excitement. Althern watched him go, a quiet pride flickering in his chest. The boy had grown in ways he hadn't anticipated, stronger, braver, and wiser. He would do well.

Turning back to Shadow, Althern crouched once more, finishing the last application of salve to the horse's legs. The stable had grown quiet again, save for the soft rustling of hay and the occasional snort from one of the other horses.

When Althern finally stepped outside, the sunlight had grown brighter, the warmth of the morning casting the city in a golden glow. The air was still, yet it thrummed with the promise of a new beginning.

"To rule is to serve," Althern muttered under his breath, the words carrying the weight of his father's lessons. "Never forget that."

Taking a deep breath, he straightened his shoulders and began walking toward the King's Hall. By the end of the day, he would no longer be a prince. He would be a king.

Chapter 37

Spring 1308 Epiris City

The bells of Epiris rang out across the city, their deep, resonant tones announcing the dawn of a new era. The streets were alive with colour and celebration, banners of white and gold fluttering from windows and balconies. Citizens dressed in their finest garments filled the square outside the King's Hall, their faces bright with hope and anticipation. The air was thick with the aroma of roasted meats, spiced wine, and fresh bread, mingling with the lively notes of minstrels' melodies drifting through the streets.

Inside the King's Hall, the transformation was breathtaking. Hundreds of candles bathed the chamber in warm light, their golden glow reflecting on the polished stone floors. Epiris's banners hung proudly from the high arches, and garlands of flowers in every colour adorned the columns, filling the air with a faint floral scent.

Althern stood at the centre of it all, clad in ceremonial armour that gleamed like molten silver. A pristine white cape draped from his shoulders, the hem brushing the polished floor. The circlet of a prince had been replaced with a simpler silver band, a temporary crown until the formal ceremony.

Surrounding him were those who had fought and bled by his side: Pesus, Bones, Ghoshte, and Daka, each dressed in their finest tunics and armour, standing as symbols of Epiris's enduring strength. Pax, now on his journey to Juntya, was the only one absent from the gathering.

The Hall was filled with a mix of nobles, knights, and dignitaries, their silks and velvets shimmering in the candlelight. But beyond its walls, the people of Epiris gathered in vast numbers, pressing into squares, peering through open windows, and filling the streets to listen. They had endured the darkness of war, and today, their unity shone brighter than ever.

The High Priestess of Epiris stepped forward, her flowing white robes edged with gold catching the candlelight as she carried the ancient crown of the kingdom. Forged centuries ago, the crown was a masterpiece, a circlet of pure gold adorned with sapphires that gleamed like captured starlight.

Althern knelt before her, the weight of the moment settling over him, not as a burden, but as a solemn vow.

"Althern Apiusson" the priestess intoned, her voice echoing through the hall with the clarity of ancient tradition, "do you swear to rule with wisdom and justice, to protect the people of this realm, and to honour the sacrifices made for this crown?"

"I swear" Althern replied, his voice steady and strong.

The priestess raised the crown high above her head. "Then rise, Althern, King of Epiris."

As the crown descended onto his head, its cool weight pressed against his brow, Althern rose to his feet. Applause and cheers thundered through the Hall, soldiers striking their swords against shields in a chorus of approval. Outside, the citizens erupted into jubilant cheers, their voices carrying on the wind.

Althern raised a hand, silencing the crowd. He stepped forward to the edge of the dais, his posture tall and regal, his voice ringing through the chamber and beyond.

"My people" he began, his tone firm yet heartfelt. "Today is not my day, it is our day. This crown does not belong to me alone. It belongs to every one of you. You fought for this city. You bled for it. You held the line when all hope seemed lost. It is because of you that we stand here, free and united."

A ripple of agreement spread through the crowd, murmurs of pride and resolve echoing back to him.

"I take this crown not to rule over you, but to serve you. A king is not a tyrant. A king is not above his people. A king is a servant of the realm."

He paused, letting the words settle. "We have endured much, betrayal, war, and great loss. Yet through it all, we proved one truth. Epiris will never fall. Not so long as we stand together. Not so long as we remember who we are."

His voice softened slightly. "Today marks the start of a new era. A time of rebuilding, healing, and honouring those who gave their lives for this kingdom. To those we have lost, we owe everything. To those still with us, we owe our strength. Together, we will forge a future worthy of their memory."

Althern raised his goblet high, his voice swelling with conviction. "To Epiris!"

The room erupted into cheers, the sound spilling into the streets, where the celebrations were already in full swing.

The city of Epiris pulsed with life and joy. In the grand square outside the King's Hall, long banquet tables stretched in rows, piled high with fruits, steaming pies, sweet breads, and bowls of delicacies. Barrels of ale and wine stood open, their contents poured freely into tankards and goblets. The rich aroma of spiced lamb, honeyed venison, and candied apples filled the air.

Minstrels wandered through the crowd, their lively tunes coaxing cheers and laughter from onlookers. A group of dancers in vibrant costumes of red, blue, and gold twirled and stomped to the music, their swirling movements drawing applause. Children wove through the throng, clutching wooden swords and sweet honeycakes as they dodged the half-hearted scolding of their parents.

Soldiers, too, joined the revelry. Their polished armour caught the warm light of torches as they swapped stories of battle and toasted their comrades. Their laughter rang out, a sharp contrast to the grim silence they had maintained during the war.

Inside the King's Hall, the mood was no less jubilant. Though more formal, the feasting and camaraderie were heartfelt. Althern sat at the head of the table, sharing quiet words and smiles with those closest to him. Bones, predictably, was at the centre of a roaring conversation, his booming laugh carrying across the room as he nudged Ghoshte, nearly spilling both their goblets of ale. Ghoshte, usually sharp and reserved, cracked a rare grin as he retorted with a dry remark that set the table roaring with laughter.

Captain Daka, seated a few chairs down, watched the scene with quiet satisfaction. His sharp eyes surveyed the room, but the hint of a smile betrayed his pride in the kingdom's newfound unity.

"Come on, Ghoshte!" Bones bellowed, slapping his friend on the back. "You've faced armies and stared down death. Surely, you can handle a second goblet of wine!"

Ghoshte smirked, raising his goblet. "I'll handle it better than you, Captain. You're spilling more than you're drinking."

The table erupted in laughter again, Bones throwing his head back. "Fair point!" he roared.

As the sun drifted across the skyline, echoes of the coronation feast still lingered faintly in the air. Cheers, laughter, and the clinking of goblets, but now the hall was quiet, its grandeur empty save for two figures. Althern sat slouched on the throne, the newly placed crown feeling heavier on his head than he had imagined. Pesus stood near the dais, arms crossed, his expression calm yet attentive.

For a moment, neither man spoke. Then, Althern let out a long, low sigh and leaned forward, resting his elbows on his knees. "It's done, Pesus. The crown's mine. The hall was full of people cheering my name... and all I could think about was how much my father's shadow still looms over me."

Pesus uncrossed his arms and stepped closer, his boots echoing faintly on the stone floor. "It's natural to feel that weight. Your father ruled for decades. No one expects you to be him."

Althern straightened, his gaze distant as he stared at the flickering torches lining the walls. "That's the problem. I don't know if I'm supposed to be him, or someone entirely different. He believed in power, in control, in making the kingdom fear him as much as they respected him. And it worked. But it also cost him. It cost all of us." He shook his head. "And now here I am, wondering if I should carry on his policies or forge my own path. If I make the wrong choice, it's not just me who suffers. It's the entire realm."

Pesus studied him for a moment before replying, his tone firm but not unkind. "You've already chosen a different path, Your Grace. Today's speech wasn't your father's words, it was yours. The people saw it. They believe in you because you're not him. You don't need to be."

Althern smiled faintly, though it didn't reach his eyes.

"You make it sound so simple. But every decision feels like a test, one I can't afford to fail."

Pesus leaned against one of the pillars near the throne, relaxing slightly, his voice softer now. "No one is ready for the weight of a crown, Althern. Not even your father, as much as he might've pretended otherwise. He made his mistakes, just like you will. But strength isn't about avoiding failure, it's about standing up after it."

Althern nodded, his jaw tightening slightly as he absorbed Pesus's words. For a moment, they sat in silence again, the crackle of the torches filling the hall. Then, hesitantly, Althern glanced at his friend, his voice dropping to a more personal tone. "There's something else. Something I haven't told anyone."

Pesus arched a brow. "Go on."

"It's Marya," Althern admitted, the name coming out almost like a confession. "I care for her, Pesus. More than I should. But how can a king be with someone like her? A healer from Garhelm? She's everything this court would sneer at. And worse, I'd be asking her to give up her life for this... for me."

Pesus didn't answer right away, instead studying Althern carefully. When he spoke, his voice was steady but laced with understanding. "You've fought battles, Althern. Hard ones. But this? This is different. A king may belong to his people, but you're still a man. If Marya is what your heart wants, you'll have to fight for her like you've fought for this kingdom. And that fight won't end with a single victory."

"And if it's a fight I can't win?" Althern asked, his voice barely above a whisper.

Pesus smiled faintly, his expression softening. "You won't know until you try. But I'll say this, you'll make a better king if your heart isn't weighed down with regrets."

Althern leaned back in the throne, his head tipping against the high back as he closed his eyes. The weight of the crown pressed against his brow, but Pesus's words settled something in his chest. "You've always had the right words, Pesus," he said quietly.

Pesus chuckled, stepping back toward the shadows of the hall. "It's a rare gift. Don't get used to it."

As the Grand Marshal turned to leave, Althern opened his eyes and watched the flickering flames along the walls. His doubts didn't vanish, but for the first time that day, he felt the faintest sense of direction. He wasn't his father. He wasn't alone. And perhaps, just perhaps, he had the strength to lead his people and himself, toward something better.

Althern stood and called for attention. "My people" he announced, his voice carrying above the crowd, "join me on the city walls at sunset. There is something I wish to share."

Curiosity rippled through the gathered crowd as they made their way to the western walls of the city. The sun was beginning to sink below the horizon, painting the plains in hues of gold and crimson. Below the walls, the seventeen surviving warhorses from the battle stood in a makeshift corral, their dark coats gleaming in the fading light.

Althern stood at the forefront of the crowd, his voice quieter now but no less commanding. "These horses fought for Epiris as fiercely as any soldier. They carried us through fire, blood, and destruction. They are not mere beasts, they are comrades. And they have earned their freedom."

With a nod, Althern signalled the stable boys to open the corral gates. The horses hesitated for a moment before trotting out onto the open plain. As they gained confidence, they broke into a gallop, their manes streaming like banners in the wind.

The crowd watched in reverent silence, the sight of the

horses running free stirring a deep sense of pride and hope. Althern turned to the people, his expression solemn.

"This plain was once a battlefield, a place of death. Today, it has become a sanctuary. These horses, like us, have endured. And like us, they deserve their freedom."

He raised a hand, his voice ringing with finality. "Let them be known as the Horses of Epiris. Let their freedom mark the dawn of a new era for our kingdom."

The applause that followed was thunderous, echoing across the city walls and out into the plains beyond.

Althern lingered as the crowd began to disperse, his gaze fixed on the silhouettes of the horses against the horizon. The image burned itself into his mind, a symbol of resilience, hope, and the promise of a brighter future.

For Epiris, the first steps toward that future had just begun.

Chapter 38

Spring 1308 Juntya Village

The early evening sun bathed the village of Juntya in a warm glow, casting long shadows over the cobbled square and the wooden houses that surrounded it. A gentle breeze carried the scents of freshly baked bread and blooming wildflowers, blending with the faint murmur of villagers finishing their day's work. That murmur shifted to hushed whispers as distant riders approached, their polished armour glinting like mirrors in the sun. At their forefront, the banner of the King fluttered boldly, its gold and white a striking contrast against the deep blue sky.

In the square, Fara paused mid-conversation with a neighbour, her heart tightening as she spotted the banner. Her hands clutched her shawl instinctively, the sight stirring memories she had tried to bury, the last time the King's banner had arrived in Juntya, it had bore bad news about her son Pax. A knot of fear twisted in her chest.

"Do you think…" Fara's voice faltered, her throat tightening. "Do you think they've come with news of Pax?"

Her neighbour placed a hand on her arm, her expression

softening. "Let's go find out, dont worry my dear" she said gently, though her own brow furrowed with worry.

The sharp clang of a hammer ceased as Eldrin, Fara's husband, stepped out of his workshop. His soot smudged hands rested on his leather apron, and his piercing gaze swept across the square. "What's going on?" he called out, his deep voice carrying easily.

Fara pointed towards the riders, her voice trembling. "It's the King's banner. Do you think… do you think it's Pesus bringing news of Pax?"

Eldrin's jaw tightened, his weathered face unreadable. He wiped his hands on his apron, drawing in a steadying breath. "Let's wait and see" he said, though his tense posture betrayed his apprehension. "It might not be anything."

But they both knew it was something.

The villagers slowly gathered, the air thick with anticipation as the cavalry entered the square. The horses moved with practiced precision, their hooves ringing against the cobblestones. At their head rode a young man, his armour immaculate and his posture straight as a blade. He dismounted with fluid grace, removing his helmet to reveal neatly cropped dark hair and a face that radiated quiet confidence.

Fara's breath caught in her throat. She stared at him, her mind racing to make sense of what she was seeing. His presence was commanding, yet there was something achingly familiar about him.

Then it hit her.

"Pax?" she whispered, her voice barely audible.

The recognition washed over her like a tidal wave. "Pax!" she cried, tears already streaming down her face as she ran towards him, her shawl fluttering behind her.

Pax turned at the sound of his name, just in time to catch his mother as she flung her arms around him. Her sobs came in heavy gasps as she clung to him, her hands grasping at his armour as though to confirm he was real.

"My boy" she wept, her voice muffled against his chest. "My boy, you're alive!"

Pax's throat tightened as he held her close, his own tears threatening to spill. "I'm home, Mother" he said softly. "I'm here."

The commotion had drawn Eldrin into the square. He froze as he saw Pax, his broad shoulders stiffening as his eyes locked onto his son. For a long moment, he didn't move, disbelief etched into his features. Then, as the reality sank in, he strode forward, his pace quickening until he reached them.

"Pax" Eldrin said, his voice thick with emotion.

Pax turned, and the moment their eyes met, the tears came. "Father."

They embraced tightly, the world around them fading into nothing. Fara joined them, her hands trembling as she brushed her son's hair and touched his face, still overwhelmed by the miracle of his return.

Pax glanced over his shoulder and gave a nod to his men, dismissing them. They rode off to set up camp at the edge of the village, leaving the square to its usual tranquillity. Pax followed his parents back to their home, his mother hurrying ahead, her tears now replaced with a flurry of activity.

"Sit, sit!" Fara insisted as she moved about the small but homely kitchen, gathering ingredients and utensils. "You must be starving. Let me get you something."

Eldrin chuckled as he sat across from Pax at the sturdy wooden table, though his hands trembled slightly as he poured water into a cup. "Fara, let the boy breathe."

"It's fine, Father" Pax said, his lips curving into a smile. "I've missed her cooking."

Fara beamed, placing a bowl of steaming broth in front of

him. As Pax ate, he began to recount his journey, his time with the cavalry, the battles he had fought, the men he had ridden with, and the moment he had been named Captain.

"And this" Pax said, unsheathing his sword and laying it on the table, "Is the blade you forged, Father. It's been with me through everything."

Eldrin reached out, his calloused hands reverently tracing the markings he had etched into the steel nearly two decades ago. His breath hitched as he turned the blade over, marvelling at its condition. "You fought with this?"

Pax nodded. "I wouldn't trust any other."

Eldrin's hands tightened around the hilt, his eyes brimming with pride. "I made this for a king," he murmured, his voice trembling. "I never imagined it would bring you back to us."

Breaking the moment, Pax reached into his satchel and pulled out a sealed scroll. "There's something else" he said, handing it to his father. "The King asked me to deliver this."

Eldrin broke the wax seal carefully, his brow furrowing as he read. His expression shifted from confusion to disbelief, then to something softer, something that spoke of long, held wounds beginning to heal.

"What is it?" Fara asked, pausing with a loaf of bread in her hands.

"It's…" Eldrin's voice cracked. "It's an apology."

"An apology?" Fara repeated, stepping closer.

Eldrin nodded, his eyes scanning the parchment again. "From King Althern. He's apologising for the decision that cost me the trade with the royal armoury. And…" He hesitated, his voice thick. "He's inviting us to move to Epiris. To become the royal armourer."

Fara gasped, her hands flying to her mouth. "Eldrin…"

"There's more," he said, his voice breaking. "He's gifting

us a horse, Shadow. The King's horse and a cart to move our things, if we want to join Pax in Epiris."

Pax's eyes widened. "I didn't know about this" he admitted, his tone just as surprised as theirs.

Fara's tears spilled anew as she hugged Eldrin tightly, her joy spilling over. "A new life in Epiris?" she whispered.

Eldrin nodded, his own tears slipping free as he smiled at her.

Without another word, Fara rushed out the door, calling for the neighbours. Eldrin followed moments later, laughing as he shouted the news to anyone who would listen.

Left alone in the house, Pax sat in silence, his hand resting on the hilt of his father's blade. The weight of the moment settled over him. King Althern, a man burdened with rebuilding a kingdom, had taken the time to right a wrong so small in the grand scheme of things.

The gesture humbled Pax. It inspired him.

For the first time in what felt like years, he allowed himself to smile, a true, unguarded smile. His parents were happy. And for now, that was all that mattered.

Chapter 39

Spring 1308 Marya's Hut

The forest buzzed with life, a chorus of chirping insects, rustling leaves and the distant calls of unseen birds. Sunlight filtered through the dense canopy above, painting dappled patterns on the narrow dirt trail. Marya led the way, her steps steady but deliberate. Arla walked just behind, her curious gaze darting between the trees, but she couldn't help noticing the slight pauses in Marya's stride. Now and then, Marya pressed a hand to her stomach, her expression momentarily distant.

"Are you all right?" Arla asked, concern softening her voice.

Marya glanced back quickly, flashing a reassuring smile. "I'm fine, Arla. Just a little tired. This old trail is rougher than I remembered."

The path wound through thick underbrush and towering trees, their roots gnarled and exposed like ancient veins creeping across the forest floor. It had been years since Marya last walked this route to the temple, yet the way was still clear in her memory.

"Why are we going to the temple today?" Arla asked, brushing a stray branch aside.

Marya glanced over her shoulder, her grin returning. "Because you've asked so many questions about the past. Sometimes, the best way to answer is to show."

The temple came into view just before midday. The forest suddenly parted, revealing a clearing dominated by an ancient stone structure. It rose solemnly from the earth, its weathered steps and dark grey stone bearing the weight of centuries. Moss clung to its surface, weaving through intricate carvings etched into the rock, scenes of warriors, priests, and animals whose features had been softened by time. Symbols with curved lines and jagged edges adorned its walls, their meaning long forgotten.

Arla stopped in her tracks, her eyes wide with awe. "It's beautiful" she breathed.

Marya nodded, her gaze soft as she took in the temple's presence. "It's more than beautiful. This is a place of stories. A place where history lingers."

She motioned for Arla to follow her closer, stepping to the temple's base where the carvings were more distinct. She pointed to a row of figures etched into the stone, men and women holding staffs, their faces weathered by time.

"These priests," Marya explained, her tone reverent, "were the keepers of knowledge. They believed the forest itself held secrets.Secrets of healing, power, and destiny. This temple was built to honour those priests."

Arla ran her fingers lightly over one of the carvings, tracing the outline of a staff. "What happened to them?"

"Time" Marya said quietly. "The priests vanished, and the forest reclaimed what was once theirs. But their stories remain, hidden in places like this."

Marya guided Arla to another section of the temple,

where a different carving caught the light. It was sharper, less weathered, as though its message had endured. At the centre of the scene stood a wolf, its sleek body carved with exquisite detail, its gaze sharp and commanding.

"This" Marya said, her voice soft with reverence, "is Amahra."

Arla tilted her head. "Amahra?"

"The White Wolf" Marya explained. "She is said to appear only in times of great need. Some believe she is a guardian angel, a protector. Others say she is a spirit of destiny itself, sent to guide the lost and nudge the world back onto its proper course."

Arla stepped closer, her breath catching as she studied the carving. The wolf seemed alive, its gaze fierce yet gentle, its presence commanding.

"I know her" Arla whispered.

Marya blinked, startled. "What do you mean?"

Arla hesitated, her hand instinctively touching the pendant around her neck a simple charm that had been given to her by her mother. Her voice was quiet, trembling slightly. "After my mother was killed in Niborya, Casius and I fled into the forest. The soldiers... they were everywhere. We didn't know where to go. And then she appeared. Amahra."

Marya's eyes widened. "You saw her?"

Arla nodded, her voice firm. "She protected us. At the stream when we were being attacked by a wild wolf. I didn't understand it then, but she saved us. Without her, we wouldn't have escaped."

Marya knelt beside Arla, her hands resting gently on the girl's shoulders. Her voice was steady, yet tinged with awe. "That's no small thing, Arla. It means something."

"She's real" Arla said, her conviction unwavering.

Marya smiled faintly. "Many stories are real, in their own

way. Many people still believe when we lose someone, that person comes back as Amahra, to look out for us and guide us" Arla pondered quietly, the last few weeks had been a steep learning curve for her.

The journey back to Marya's cabin was slower, the afternoon heat settling over the forest like a heavy blanket. Arla, her curiosity sparked, asked question after question about the plants they passed along the trail. Marya, her tone warm and patient, identified each one with care.

"That one" Marya said, pointing to a cluster of delicate white flowers, "Is feverroot. Its petals can be brewed into a tea to bring down a fever."

Arla nodded thoughtfully. "And that?" she asked, gesturing to a low-growing shrub with waxy leaves.

"Groundleaf" Marya replied. "Crush its leaves into a poultice for cuts and scrapes. It stings a little, but it works."

Their conversation flowed easily as they made their way through the forest, but as they neared the cabin, Marya spotted a commotion ahead. The sound of hooves echoed through the trees, and a group of riders circled near the stone dais, their armour catching the fading light.

Marya's breath quickened. For a moment, she thought it might be Althern. But as the riders drew closer, she recognised the banner flying from the lead rider's lance, it was not Althern, but someone in his service.

The riders dismounted in the clearing. The young man at their head introduced himself as Pax, his tone formal yet kind. He quickly informed Marya of Althern's ascension to the throne.

"King Althern" Marya murmured, her voice a mix of surprise and quiet pride.

Pax smiled and handed her a scroll sealed with the royal crest. "I've been sent with a message, Marya."

Marya took the scroll, her fingers brushing the seal before she broke it. Her eyes scanned the words, her expression softening as she read.

"What does it say?" Arla asked, stepping closer.

Marya folded the scroll carefully, her lips curving into a small smile. "It's an invitation. Althern wishes for me to visit Epiris."

Arla's face lit up. "You're going?"

Marya nodded, her gaze thoughtful. "Yes. I think I will."

She turned back to Pax, inclining her head. "Congratulations on your promotion, Captain. And thank you for bringing this."

Pax bowed slightly. "It was my honour."

As the riders began setting up camp nearby, Marya stood at the edge of the clearing, her thoughts swirling. She glanced at Arla, who knelt by a patch of feverroot, inspecting its petals with quiet fascination. The girl had been through so much, yet there was a lightness in her now. A resilience that gave Marya hope.

The forest around them buzzed softly with life as the setting sun cast long, golden shadows across the trail. Marya's gaze drifted to the horizon, her mind turning to the White Wolf and its legend.

"Amahra" she murmured under her breath. "What do you see for us?"

The wolf's presence felt closer now, its story no longer just words etched in stone. Destiny, Marya realised, was stirring once again.

Chapter 40

Spring 1308 Epiris

The late afternoon wore on as the streets bristled with activity in Epiris. Merchants called out from their stalls, hawking everything from ripe fruits to polished trinkets, while children darted through the throng, their laughter ringing out above the hum of conversation. Wagon wheels creaked as they rolled along the cobblestones, and the occasional clatter of hooves signalled the arrival of mounted messengers weaving skilfully through the crowds.

Near the heart of the city, a modest but lively tavern stood proudly, its newly repaired sign swaying gently in the breeze. Inside, Captain Daka sat by the open window, a tankard of ale in hand, his sharp eyes scanning the passersby with the easy demeanour of a man at peace. His presence didn't go unnoticed. Locals passing by often paused to nod or exchange greetings.

"Afternoon, Captain!" called a young boy carrying a basket of bread. "Good to see you still around!"

"And still standing" Daka replied with a wry grin, raising his tankard in a mock toast.

An older woman paused outside the window, her arms

laden with a basket of freshly washed linens. "Captain Daka" she teased, shaking her head, "don't let that ale go straight to your head. You've had your share of battles, but a drunken soldier's no use to anyone."

Daka chuckled, tipping an imaginary hat. "Not to worry, Matron. I've retired from wobbling about. These days, I'm just here to enjoy the scenery."

The woman laughed and continued on her way, leaving Daka to his quiet vigil by the window. He took another sip from his tankard, the faint tang of hops lingering on his tongue, when the sound of heavy boots crunching on cobblestones caught his attention. He glanced up just as Grand Marshal Pesus strode past the tavern, his broad shoulders and commanding presence instantly recognisable even without the gleam of his usual armour.

Pesus halted mid-step when he spotted Daka, a broad grin breaking across his rugged face. "Well, well" he said, stepping into the doorway. "Look at this, a man of great leisure. I didn't realise you'd gone part-time, Daka."

Daka smirked, leaning back in his chair. "I've earned it, Pesus. Can't let you hog all the peace and quiet while you're out stomping around the city on patrols."

Pesus stepped inside, waving off the barkeep's offer of a drink before settling into the chair opposite Daka. "Peace and quiet?" Pesus scoffed, crossing his arms. "You've never let anyone have peace and quiet. Frankly, I'm surprised they haven't thrown you out of here for causing a racket."

Daka barked a laugh, shaking his head. "Funny you should say that. Turns out, they can't throw me out anymore."

Pesus raised an eyebrow, intrigued. "Oh? And why's that? You charm them into tolerating you?"

"Better than that," Daka replied, his grin widening. "I bought the place."

Pesus blinked, momentarily caught off guard. "You did what?"

Daka took a deliberate sip of his ale, clearly relishing Pesus's reaction. "After the battle, the tavern was in rough shape, broken windows, smashed furniture, roof leaking like a sieve. The owners couldn't afford the repairs, not after everything that happened. So, I stepped in and made an investment."

Pesus leaned back, eyeing Daka with mock disbelief. "You? An investor? I never thought I'd see the day."

"It works for everyone," Daka said with a shrug. "The couple who owned it get to keep their livelihood.They still run the place and live upstairs. I footed the repair bills, and in return, I get a steady income and a quiet corner to drink in peace. Call it my retirement fund."

Pesus shook his head, chuckling. "The King's captains turning into tavern moguls. What's the world coming to?"

"Better than me causing trouble elsewhere," Daka shot back. "Besides, someone's got to keep an eye on you when you finally admit you're too old for the Grand Marshal's job."

Pesus snorted, gesturing toward Daka's tankard. "Just don't drink all your profits, or this brilliant little enterprise of yours won't last the year."

The banter faded as a more serious expression crossed Pesus's face. He adjusted his position, leaning forward slightly. Daka noticed the shift and tilted his head.

"What about you?" Daka asked, his tone matching Pesus's. "What's next for the Grand Marshal?"

Pesus exhaled, running a hand over his jaw. "I expect I'll be sent east soon. Patrols along the border near the Blackridge Mountains."

Daka frowned, setting his tankard down. "Rok's old kingdom?"

Pesus nodded grimly. "And beyond. Althern doesn't want to take any chances. There's been talk. Caravans coming through with whispers about men moving along the mountain passes. No one's sure if they're mercenaries, refugees, or something worse."

"You think Asos is behind it?" Daka asked, his expression hardening.

"Hard to say," Pesus replied, his tone guarded. "The man's kept quiet for years. But with Rok gone and the border less secure, he might see an opportunity. Althern's not going to sit and wait to find out."

"Smart" Daka said, nodding. "Better to know what's coming before it lands on your doorstep."

Pesus's gaze grew distant for a moment before he stood, adjusting the belt of his tunic. "Well, I'll leave you to your business empire, Captain. Just try not to turn every tavern in Epiris into part of your kingdom."

Daka grinned, raising his tankard in a mock toast. "And don't go getting yourself killed in Blackridge, Pesus. This place wouldn't be half as entertaining without your sour mug strolling past."

Pesus chuckled, clapping Daka on the shoulder as he turned to leave. "Take care, Daka. And try not to drink yourself into poverty."

As Pesus strode back out into the bustling street, Daka leaned back in his chair, watching the crowd through the open window. Merchants shouted their wares, children darted between wagons, and life in Epiris moved on, undeterred by the scars of recent battles.

Daka felt at ease, he breathed deeply, enjoying the moment. The storm had passed, and for now, he was content to sit back and let the world turn at least until the next one arrived.

Chapter 41

Spring 1308 Epiris

The golden hues of the lowering sun bathed the streets of Epiris in a warm, honeyed glow. Shadows stretched long across the cobblestones, softening the bustle of the city as it prepared for the evening. Merchants packed away their wares into carts, street vendors shouted their final offers of the day, and children darted between the adults, their laughter a lively counterpoint to the mellow hum of activity.

Althern and Marya strolled together, blending seamlessly into the city's rhythm. Though he wore no crown and his attire was modest, a deep blue tunic and finely tailored trousers, his presence commanded quiet respect. Those who passed by recognised their king, offering nods or murmured greetings. By contrast, Marya moved with understated grace, her simple dress and healer's pouch marking her as someone of quiet purpose rather than grandeur.

"Epiris has changed since I was last here" Marya said, her eyes wandering over the faces of the bustling crowd and the tall stone facades of the buildings. "There's so much life in it now. It feels as if the city is breathing again."

Althern smiled faintly. "It's mending. Slowly, but surely." He gestured towards a pair of masons repairing a crumbled wall. "There's no shortage of work for anyone. Every day, the city feels a little more like home."

"And you?" Marya asked, glancing sideways at him. "Does it feel like home for you yet?"

Althern paused mid-step, his expression thoughtful. "It's strange. I was born here, but it never truly felt like my place. Not until now."

Marya returned his smile, but she didn't press further. Instead, her gaze drifted down the street, where laughter and the faint neighing of horses carried from the direction of the stables.

The warm smell of hay and horses greeted them as they entered. Inside, Pax stood in the centre of the stable, brushing down a tall, dapple-grey mare. On the other side of the same horse, Arla worked diligently on its legs with a smaller brush, her tongue sticking out slightly as she focused.

"Gentle strokes" Pax instructed patiently. "You're doing fine, but don't rush it. The horses can sense when you're in a hurry, and they won't like it."

Casius, standing by the next stall, was far less disciplined. He held a brush in one hand and a carrot in the other, awkwardly trying to bribe his horse into standing still. "Come on, just give me a minute, will you?" he muttered as the horse flicked its ears at him, unimpressed.

"Don't give it the carrot yet!" Pax called over, exasperated. "You'll spoil the training if you keep bribing it too early."

"I'm not bribing," Casius shot back defensively, though his hand hovered perilously close to the horse's mouth.

"You're hopeless" Pax muttered, shaking his head, but there was a grin tugging at his lips.

"Looks like someone's been promoted from cavalry captain to stable master" Althern said good-humouredly as he stepped further inside, his voice carrying easily across the stable.

Pax turned, his face lighting up in a grin. "Your Grace! Marya!" He offered a quick bow, though his casual tone remained unchanged. "Figured someone had to whip these two into shape. Otherwise, they'd be terrorising the horses instead of grooming them."

Marya laughed as she approached. "You're doing well with them, Pax. Arla looks like a natural."

"She is" Pax replied, nodding towards Arla, who grinned sheepishly. "This one" he added, jerking a thumb at Casius, "still thinks the horses work for him, not the other way around."

"I heard that!" Casius shot back, his grin betraying his lack of offence.

Althern chuckled, then turned to Pax. "We're taking two horses out for a ride," he said simply.

Pax's grin faded slightly, replaced by a look of mild concern. "Do you want me to send some men with you? It's getting late—"

"No need" Althern interrupted, his tone kind but resolute. "Keep this low-key."

Pax shrugged, his grin returning. "Suit yourself, Your Grace. Don't let the horses run off with you."

Althern smirked. "And don't let these two run off with you!."

Pax laughed, already turning back to Arla and Casius. "You heard the king. Back to work!"

The city gates groaned open as Althern and Marya rode out. Their horses' hooves clicked softly against the stone path before transitioning to the muffled crunch of dirt and grass. The plains stretched wide before them, bathed in the warm glow of the setting sun. Waves of golden grass swayed gently in the breeze, and in the distance, the silhouettes of the freed warhorses moved like shadows against the horizon.

"There" Althern said, pointing to a group of horses galloping across the far ridge near the forest edge. Their dark coats shone in the light, their movements fluid and untamed.

"They look happy" Marya said softly, her voice tinged with admiration. "Do they ever come back to the stables?"

"Sometimes," Althern replied. "But only if they want to. They've earned their freedom."

Marya smiled faintly, watching the horses as they rode on. The sight stirred something within her, a quiet gratitude for the small, noble gestures that hinted at the man Althern truly was.

The forest rose ahead of them, its tall trees standing like sentinels. As they entered the cool shade, the sounds of the plains gave way to rustling leaves and the occasional call of a bird.

Althern slowed his horse as they approached a clearing. Marya followed his gaze and saw them, four massive stone statues arranged in a circle, their weathered faces gazing outward. Each figure held a sword resting tip down at their feet, their carved features regal and commanding even after centuries of erosion.

"They're incredible" Marya murmured, dismounting to get a closer look.

"They're called the Kings of Epiris" Althern explained, joining her. "Each one faces a different direction north, south, east, and west. The story goes that they were the first protectors of Epiris, watching over the kingdom from all sides."

Marya traced her fingers along the base of one statue,

feeling the grooves of its carvings. "And what happens if they're needed again?"

"The legend says they'll rise from the stone," Althern said, his tone reverent yet sceptical, "when Epiris is in its darkest hour."

Marya raised an eyebrow, a small smile playing at her lips. "Convenient story to keep the people hopeful."

"Maybe" Althern said with a chuckle. "Or maybe it's a reminder that even in dark times, someone is always watching."

They sat on a fallen log nearby, letting the quiet of the forest envelop them. Althern leaned forward, his elbows resting on his knees, his gaze distant.

"The city's recovering" he said at last. "The people are healing. The soldiers are training again. Everything feels like it's moving in the right direction."

"But?" Marya prompted gently.

He sighed. "But it's exhausting. There's always more to do, always another decision waiting."

"You're doing well," Marya said, her voice firm but kind. "Better than most would. But you don't have to carry it all alone."

"I know" he admitted quietly.

They sat in silence until Marya broke it again. "Arla's progressing quickly. She's got a natural gift for healing and a curiosity that never seems to end. But there's something else about her."

"What do you mean?"

"She's being guided," Marya said simply. "By Amahra. I can feel it. There's something about her we don't fully understand yet."

As the last light faded, they stood and walked back

towards their horses. Marya reached for Althern's hand, lacing her fingers with his.

"What does you being king mean for us?" she asked quietly.

Althern turned to her, his brow furrowing slightly. "What do you mean?"

"I mean this" she said, gesturing between them. "You're a king now. You have duties, expectations. Where do I fit into that?"

He stopped, his expression softening. "Marya, nothing has changed for me. I still feel the same."

Relief flickered across her face. "You mean that?"

"Of course" he said. "But would you ever consider living in Epiris?"

She hesitated, glancing towards the trees. "I don't know. Garhelm is home. It's where I learned everything I know."

Althern nodded slowly. "I wouldn't ask you to give that up unless it's what you wanted."

She leaned in, pressing a soft kiss to his lips. "We'll figure it out" she said.

As they mounted their horses and rode back through the forest, the air seemed to shift. Hidden in the underbrush, white eyes gleamed briefly, watching them before vanishing into the dark.

Chapter 42

Spring 1308 Epiris

The dawn broke over Epiris. A crisp breeze swept through the streets, carrying with it the faint scent of dew-laden grass from the plains beyond the gates. The air was charged with anticipation, a quiet hum growing louder as the city began to stir.

People gathered early, lining the cobblestone streets, their faces a mix of pride and worry. The grand procession of Epiris's patrol army was set to depart, bound for the eastern borderlands near the Blackridge Mountains. Rumours of troop movements had reached the King's ears, and now his forces would march to confront the unknown.

At the gates of the city, the army of Epiris stood assembled in disciplined lines. Their polished armour caught the first light of dawn, shimmering like molten silver. Above them, the King's banners fluttered in the wind, commanding reverence and inspiring hope.

At the head of the formation sat Grand Marshal Pesus, a figure of sheer authority. His battle-worn armour, though polished, bore the scars of countless campaigns. A testament to his years of service. His rounded shoulders and upright posture exuded an air of unshakable command. The white plume of his helm swayed gently in the breeze, while his grey cloak, trimmed with gold, flowed behind him like a standard.

Pesus's sharp gaze swept over the ranks with the precision of a commander who missed nothing. His deep-set eyes lingered momentarily on each unit, silently gauging their readiness. Every inch of him embodied discipline and strength. A leader his soldiers would follow without hesitation.

Just behind Pesus, Captain Bones stood among the front rankers. If Pesus was the image of discipline, Bones was raw, brute force personified. His enormous frame seemed to dwarf the men around him, his heavy plate armour appearing almost strained against his broad chest and arms. His face, a map of white scars etched into rugged features, spoke of a life lived on the edge of battle. His unconventional, two-handed sword jutted from its scabbard on his back, as if it weighed nothing.

The front rankers, mostly recruits, marched beside him with shields strapped across their backs and light swords at their sides. These were men who aspired to make it to coveted Knight of Epiris status, prepared to stand in the first line of the next fight. Their grim faces reflected both resolve and readiness, while the rhythmic clank of their boots on the stone echoed like the steady beat of a war drum.

Bones turned his head slightly, catching the gaze of a young boy waving enthusiastically from the crowd. A rare grin softened his stern features, and he raised a gauntleted hand in a casual salute. The boy's face lit up, his excitement bubbling over as his father ruffled his hair with a chuckle.

To the right of the column, Captain Pax rode at the head of the cavalry. His polished armour gleamed in the morning light, the silver sheen offset by a grey sash tied diagonally across his chest, a mark of his captaincy.

Pax's youthful face held a calm, measured focus that belied his years, though there remained a flicker of wonder in his eyes as he glanced at the cheering crowd. His horse, a sleek brown stallion with a polished coat, moved with an elegant yet powerful gait, its hooves clicking smartly against the cobblestones.

Behind Pax, the cavalry rode two abreast, their lances upright and pennants snapping sharply in the breeze. The steady thunder of their hooves mingled with the metallic clinking of bridles and the occasional snort of a restless horse. The precision of their formation and the discipline in their bearing were a testament to rigorous training. Their presence exuded confidence and strength, drawing admiration from the gathered townsfolk.

Further back in the procession, Captain Ghoshte led the archers with quiet authority. His lean frame moved with the fluid grace of a predator, every step purposeful. His dark, piercing eyes scanned the crowd, reading it as easily as one might read a well-worn map. His brown leather armour, trimmed with subtle green accents, marked him as a master of forest warfare. A curved bow rested over his shoulder, its string taut and ready.

Walking beside him was Casius, who, despite his youth, carried himself with an air of burgeoning confidence. His plain tunic and sturdy boots set him apart from the officers, but the respect he had earned was evident in the subtle nods and glances from the archers as they passed.

The archers moved with quiet precision, their quivers swaying lightly against their backs. These were men who could rain death upon an enemy from great distances, felling foes long before the clash of blades. Their calm, focused demeanour added a sharp edge to the procession. A reminder that wars were won as much from afar as in the thick of combat.

Among the knights marched a new figure. Captain Lucian. Recently promoted, he carried himself with the stiff formality of someone not yet comfortable in his role. His armour, pristine and polished to a near blinding shine, was almost too perfect and the white plume on his helm marked him as a leader among the knights.

Lucian's youthful face, serious and intent, betrayed the weight of his new responsibility. His sharp features and piercing blue eyes gave him an air of intelligence, though his movements lacked the effortless confidence of veterans like Ghoshte or Bones. He marched with his gaze fixed forward, determined to meet the expectations placed upon him.

As he passed, whispers rippled through the crowd, curiosity sparking about the young captain who had joined the patrol army.

From the city walls above, King Althern stood watching, his hands resting lightly on the cool stone battlements. His finely made but simple tunic shifted slightly in the morning breeze, the deep blue fabric catching the light.

The gathered crowd below caught sight of him, and a cheer rose like a wave, rolling through the streets. Their voices carried upward, a sound that was both reverent and triumphant.

Althern raised a hand in acknowledgment, his expression warm but solemn. His gaze followed the procession as it moved through the gates. Pesus, at the forefront, cut an imposing figure, his armour catching the sun like a beacon. Bones followed, his massive frame and scarred face as much a symbol of resilience as the banners that flew overhead.

Pax rode proudly with his cavalry, the silver gleam of his

armour matched only by the discipline of the riders behind him. Ghoshte's archers marched with quiet precision, their bows a silent promise of protection. Even Captain Lucian, with his nervous energy, carried himself with an undeniable dignity.

As the last ranks passed through the gates, Althern remained on the battlements, watching the army move as one towards the horizon. His heart swelled with a mix of pride and apprehension. Though the city behind him had begun to heal, the road ahead for his men was fraught with uncertainty. He was used to being able to ride out with his men, but Epiris needed him... And he trusted Pesus, he knew the army was in good hands.

For now, the people cheered. For now, the army marched. And for now, the King hoped that their unity would be enough to face whatever lay in the shadow of the Blackridge Mountains.

CHAPTER 43

SUMMER 1308 EPIRIS

The forest beyond Epiris was alive with the sounds of early morning. Birds called from the canopy above, their songs weaving a melodic backdrop to the crunch of hooves and boots on the forest floor. The air was cool and damp, carrying the earthy scent of moss and fallen leaves. Althern rode at the front of the small hunting party, his eyes scanning the undergrowth for signs of movement.

Beside him, Daka handled his horse with the ease of a man who had spent much of his life in the wild. He had traded his usual armour for a lighter leather jerkin, though the broad blade at his side was as menacing as ever. Behind them, Captain Beran of the King's Guard rode with four cavalrymen, their spears held loosely but ready for action.

"You'll scare off the prey with all that clanking" Daka said, throwing a pointed glance at the armoured guards behind them.

"They're cavalry, Daka, not shadows" Althern replied with a smirk. "Subtlety isn't exactly part of the job description."

"Well, they'd better learn" Daka grumbled, nudging his horse forward. "A boar won't stop and wait for you to unbuckle your armour."

Beran snorted, his expression impassive. "The boar doesn't need to wait. I'll catch it before it goes far."

Daka twisted in his saddle, grinning. "Careful, Captain. Confidence like that tends to end with someone flat on their back."

Beran raised an eyebrow. "Not today."

It wasn't long before the group found evidence of their quarry. Deep hoofprints pressed into the damp earth, tufts of coarse fur snagged on low branches, and fresh marks where the animal had rooted for food.

"This way" Daka said, sliding from his horse. He crouched by the tracks, running his fingers over the disturbed soil. "It's fresh. Not more than thirty minutes ahead of us."

Althern dismounted, his boots sinking slightly into the soft ground. He gestured for the cavalry to hold their position at the edge of the forest. "Stay here. If the boar doubles back, signal us."

Beran nodded, though his sharp eyes scanned the surrounding trees, as if expecting more than just wildlife.

Althern and Daka moved deeper into the woods, their footsteps careful and deliberate. The canopy thickened, filtering sunlight into shifting patterns on the forest floor.

"This reminds me of the hunts with your father," Daka said, his voice low. "Though he was always better with a bow than you."

Althern huffed a laugh. "He had more time to practise. I've been a little busy trying to keep the kingdom from falling apart."

Daka smirked. "Excuses. You'll never match him if you keep blaming the crown."

The boar appeared without warning, bursting from a dense thicket with a guttural grunt and a flash of bristling fur. Its hulking frame tore through the undergrowth with surprising speed, tusks gleaming as it charged.

"There!" Daka shouted, drawing his sword as the animal veered away.

Althern's heart pounded as they gave chase, branches whipping past as the forest blurred around them. The boar moved with remarkable agility, weaving through the trees and leading them into a sunlit clearing. They stumbled to a halt, their breaths heavy in the sudden stillness.

But the boar was gone.

"Where did it—" Daka began, his question cut short as his eyes landed on the clearing's centre.

There, standing where the boar should have been, was something neither of them expected.

The white wolf of Amahra.

Its shimmering coat glowed faintly in the sunlight, its fur so pristine it seemed almost ethereal. Its piercing eyes, white as snow, locked onto Althern with an unsettling intensity. The wolf stood impossibly still, its presence more like that of a spectre than a creature of the forest.

"What in the—" Daka's voice faltered as he drew his sword instinctively. With a swift motion, he swung the blade in a wide arc and the steel passed through the wolf as if it were nothing but mist.

Daka staggered, his eyes wide. "What kind of sorcery is this?"

"Stop" Althern ordered, his voice steady and commanding. "Put your sword away. It's Amahra."

Daka hesitated, his grip tightening on the hilt. But at last, he sheathed the blade, muttering under his breath. "If it's a spirit, it could've warned us before scaring the life out of us."

The wolf's gaze never wavered from Althern. When it spoke, its voice was low and resonant, filling the clearing like the rumble of distant thunder.

"An enemy stirs in the lands beyond the Blackridge Mountains" it said. "A force musters, and one who was once an ally has been turned by someone you once trusted. If you do not act, your kingdom will fall and the cost will be greater than you can bear."

Althern's brows drew together in a frown as he stepped closer. "Who is this ally? Who turned them?"

The wolf's eyes seemed to gleam brighter. "You will know in time."

Althern opened his mouth to speak again, but the wolf interrupted, its voice cutting through the silence like a blade.

"Your son will not survive if you fail."

The words hit him like a physical blow. He froze, his breath catching. "I don't have a son" he said, his voice low and uncertain.

The wolf ignored his protest, turning away. Its shimmering form began to dissolve, fading like mist into the shadows of the forest.

"Wait!" Althern called, taking a step forward. "What did you mean? Who—"

The wolf was gone.

For a moment, neither man spoke. The forest around them seemed eerily quiet, as if holding its breath.

"A son?" Daka said finally, his tone cautious but curious. "Have you... been with Marya?"

Althern turned to him, his expression a mix of frustration and bewilderment. "That's not—" He stopped, the wolf's words echoing in his mind. Could it be true? His relationship with Marya had been fleeting but undeniable.

If it were true, the revelation filled him with both an unexpected joy and a sharp, gnawing fear.

"If it is true…" Althern murmured, almost to himself, "then everything just became far more complicated."

Daka clapped a hand on his shoulder, his expression unusually serious. "It's not the end of the world. But you'd better be ready to fight for both your kingdom and your family."

They returned to the forest's edge, where Captain Beran and the cavalry waited. The soldiers stood around the massive body of the boar, its lifeless form sprawled in a pool of blood.

Beran glanced up as they approached, his expression calm but satisfied. "It ran straight into us. Didn't even get a chance to turn."

"Good work" Althern said distractedly, his thoughts clearly elsewhere.

Beran frowned slightly. "Is everything all right, Your Grace?"

Althern nodded absently, mounting his horse. "Yes. Let's bring the boar back to the city."

As they rode through the forest, Althern's mind replayed the wolf's warning, its words like a dark refrain.

An enemy. A trusted betrayer. A son.

Each phrase weighed heavily on him, but the thought of a child, his child, pressed most on his heart. If the wolf spoke the truth, his every action from this moment forward would mean the difference between survival and ruin. Not just for Epiris, but for a family he might not have known he had.

The trees began to thin as the party neared the city, the towering walls of Epiris rising from the horizon like a bastion of stone and strength. Yet, even as the familiar sight of home came into view, the questions stirred by the wolf's warning remained unanswered, looming like shadows over Althern's thoughts.

Chapter 44

Summer 1308 Epiris

The pub was alive with laughter and music, the hum of conversation filling every corner of the cosy establishment. The fire in the hearth crackled warmly, casting a golden glow over the room and mingling with the soft light of lanterns strung from the ceiling beams. The scent of cooking food and freshly baked bread wafted through the air, mixing with the tang of spilled ale and the faint sweetness of honeyed mead.

Arla darted between the tables, a cloth in one hand and an empty tankard in the other. Her blonde hair bounced as she moved, her face flushed from the heat of the room and the thrill of the evening. She laughed as one of the patrons, an older man with a bushy beard, called out for more ale. "Coming right up!" she chirped, her voice light and melodic.

From his spot behind the bar, Daka watched her with a faint smile. She was good for the place, her youthful energy lifting the spirits of even the most dour customers. He'd never intended for her to work here, but she'd insisted on helping out, saying she wanted to feel useful. He supposed with Casius gone with the army and Marya busy with the King,

Arla probably just wanted somewhere familiar. She was great for the place. The regulars adored her, and the pub's atmosphere had grown lighter since she'd started.

But Daka's smile faded as his sharp eyes caught something unsettling. At a table near the corner, a man—tall and lean with a scruffy beard and hooded cloak was leaning too close to Arla. His hand hovered near her arm, and his grin was too wide, too familiar. Arla, ever polite, stepped back and kept wiping the table, her cheerful demeanour not faltering.

The man's hand reached out, taking hold of her wrist.

Daka was moving before he even realised it, his heavy boots thudding against the wooden floor. "Oi" he growled, his deep voice cutting through the din of the room. The pub quieted slightly, heads turning to see what was happening.

The man looked up, his grin faltering as he met Daka's glare. "Just having a chat" he said, raising his hands as if in innocence.

Daka loomed over him, his presence as imposing as a thundercloud. "You're done chatting. Out. Now."

The man hesitated, glancing around the room as though searching for support. But the other patrons looked away, their expressions wary. No one crossed Daka.

Without a word, the man rose to his feet. Daka grabbed him by the collar and half-dragged him toward the door. "You so much as look at her again, and I'll break both your legs" Daka snarled as he shoved him outside. The door slammed shut behind him, the sound echoing through the pub.

"Who was that?" Daka demanded, turning to the pub's landlord and landlady, who were standing behind the bar.

They exchanged uneasy glances. "Never seen him before" the landlord admitted, scratching his head. "Didn't look like one of the usuals."

Daka's frown deepened, but he nodded and returned to his

place behind the bar. He kept his eyes on Arla for the rest of the evening, his instincts on edge.

Arla, however, seemed unbothered. She continued clearing tables, her cheerful mood undimmed. A while later, someone called out for a song, and she laughed, wiping her hands on her apron. "All right, all right" she said, climbing onto a stool near the hearth.

The room quieted as she began to sing, her voice clear and sweet. The song was an old one, about the hunt and the creatures of the forest. A tune her mother had taught her long ago. The melody wove through the air like a spell, the words painting vivid images of deer darting through the trees, of foxes hiding in their dens, and of the thrill of the chase. Her voice seemed to brighten the room even further, and when she finished, the patrons erupted into applause, cheering and pounding their tankards on the tables.

Arla blushed, laughing as she hopped down from the stool. "You're too kind" she said, bowing theatrically before returning to her work.

As the evening wore on, the pub gradually emptied. The regulars said their goodnights, and the room grew quieter. Arla hummed softly to herself as she wiped down the last of the tables, her mood still buoyant.

"I just need to get something to eat" she called to Daka, who was stacking chairs near the bar.

"All right," he said, glancing up briefly. "Don't take too long."

She flashed him a grin and disappeared through the door that led to the back room. The door swung shut behind her, the sound barely noticeable over the crackle of the fire.

Daka finished stacking the chairs, his mind still replaying the events of earlier. Something about that man didn't sit right with him. He hadn't liked the way he'd looked at Arla, the way he'd lingered too long.

A few minutes passed, and he realised he hadn't heard anything from Arla.

"Arla?" he called, heading toward the back room. There was no response.

Frowning, he pushed open the door. The room was dark, the faint moonlight from the high window casting long shadows across the walls. The air was cold, much colder than it should have been. The door leading to the outside stood ajar, swaying slightly in the wind.

"Arla?" he said again, louder this time. His voice echoed in the empty space.

He stepped forward, his heart pounding. Something caught his eye near the doorframe. A strip of fabric fluttered in the breeze, snagged on a splintered edge of wood. He reached out and took it, his stomach twisting as he recognised the pattern. It was from Arla's dress.

The door banged loudly against the frame, the sound making him jump. He stepped outside, his breath fogging in the cold night air. The forest loomed dark and silent beyond the clearing, its shadows deep and impenetrable.

"Arla!" he shouted, his voice raw. The only response was the rustling of leaves and the distant hoot of an owl.

Panic surged through him, sharp and overwhelming. He turned back to the pub, his mind racing.

"She's gone" he muttered, his voice barely audible. His hands clenched into fists, the strip of fabric crumpling in his grasp. The memory of her laughter, her singing, her bright smile flashed through his mind, each image twisting the knife deeper.

Daka leaned against the doorframe, his breaths coming in

short, ragged gasps. He'd promised to protect her, to keep her safe. And now she was gone.

The landlord and landlady rushed to Daka's side to see what the commotion was. As Daka explained, whilst walking out onto the cobbles behind the pub, the landlady cried in shock. An abduction, in her pub. Somewhere out there, Arla was alone, afraid, and in danger. The thought was unbearable.

"I'll find you," he swore, his voice low and fierce. "I'll bring you back."

But even as he spoke the words, a cold dread settled in his chest. He had no idea where to start, no trail to follow. And the night seemed to stretch endlessly before him, dark and unforgiving.

Chapter 45

Summer 1308 Epiris

The forest trail snaked through the trees like a ribbon, its twists and turns dappled with sunlight breaking through the dense canopy above. Grand Marshal Pesus rode at the head of the column, his grey cloak trailing behind him, its edges dusted from the long march. His armour caught the occasional glint of the morning light, the battered yet polished plates a testament to countless battles fought and survived.

Behind him stretched the disciplined ranks of Epiris's army. Their measured steps formed a steady rhythm, the muffled crunch of boots and the occasional clink of metal echoing softly through the tranquil woods.

The morning air was crisp, carrying the earthy scent of the forest. Birds darted between branches, their melodic calls weaving through the hum of the army's march. Yet, for all its beauty, the forest felt unnaturally quiet, as though it too held its breath, anticipating the danger that lay ahead.

Pesus's sharp eyes roamed the path ahead, his senses heightened. Though the woods appeared calm, he trusted neither their stillness nor the unseen shadows that could conceal ambushes.

"Grand Marshal!" came the familiar gruff voice of Captain Bones from behind. The massive warrior urged his equally imposing warhorse closer, the pair an intimidating sight. Bones's armour, though lighter than a usual soldiers, still seemed to strain against his immense frame. His two-handed sword, strapped across his back, jutted out like a second spine.

"I still don't know why you insist I ride one of these blasted things" Bones muttered, flicking the reins toward his horse. The animal responded with an irritated shake of its head, nearly unseating him as he tipped forward in the saddle.

"See? I'm more likely to die on this thing than in battle."

Pesus chuckled at his friend's predicament. For all his skill as a captain, Bones had never quite developed the officer's decorum expected of him.

"You're an officer, Bones. I can't have you turning up for a fight covered head to toe in dirt and grime, looking like you've walked the length of the kingdom, can I?"

Bones grumbled under his breath, adjusting the reins and shifting uncomfortably in the saddle. A companionable silence fell between them as they rode on, the warmth of the afternoon sun softening the tension of the moment.

"You look tense" Bones remarked, his voice tinged with amusement.

Pesus didn't turn. "We're too exposed. I'd rather be tense than dead."

Bones let out a low chuckle. "Fair enough. But I wouldn't mind a skirmish, keeps the men sharp, especially with these new replacements."

Pesus allowed himself the faintest smile. "Careful what you wish for."

As they continued, the trees began to thin, revealing the outskirts of a small village. Niborya. Pesus raised his hand, the universal signal for the column to halt.

The soldiers stopped in unison, their armour clinking softly as they shifted in place. The village ahead was a shadow of its former self. Once bustling with life, it now bore the scars of its recent attack. Only a handful of houses had been rebuilt, their thatched roofs uneven and patched with mismatched timber. Smoke rose lazily from a few chimneys, faint signs of life amidst the ruins.

Villagers peered cautiously from doorways and windows, their faces weathered and lined with fear and resilience. Some simply stood in silence, while others whispered nervously as the soldiers filled the streets.

Pesus turned to Bones. "We'll rest here briefly. Let the men refill their water at the well and check their gear."

Bones dismounted with a grunt, gesturing for the front rankers to follow. "All right, you heard him! Fill your canteens and keep sharp."

Toward the rear of the column, Casius, walking alongside the archers, paused as his eyes locked onto a small, weathered house near the edge of the village. His steps faltered, and, without a word, he handed his bow to Ghoshte before heading toward the dwelling.

The house stood quiet, its doorway covered by a simple curtain of coarse fabric. The sagging roof and weathered walls hinted at years of neglect, yet it remained standing. Casius stepped onto the creaking porch, pushing aside the curtain to enter.

Inside, the air was stale, carrying the faint scent of smoke and old memories. Sunlight filtered through gaps in the walls, illuminating broken furniture scattered across the floor, a chair missing a leg, a warped table ruined by leaks.

As he moved through the room, his boots stirred the thick dust. Near the hearth, his gaze fell on a small wooden carving lying on the floor. He crouched, picking it up. It was a simple figurine of a horse, its edges smooth from years of handling.

Emotion welled within him, not the fiery rage that had driven him for so long, but a deep, aching sorrow. He could almost hear his mother's laughter, faint and fleeting, like a memory slipping through his grasp.

"I got my revenge" he murmured, his voice steady but heavy. "But it doesn't bring you back."

"Casius."

He turned to see Ghoshte standing in the doorway, his expression unreadable.

"We're moving out" Ghoshte said quietly.

Casius nodded, placing the carving gently back on the floor. As he stepped outside, he gave the house one last glance before following Ghoshte.

The forest eventually gave way to open plains, the trees thinning until the sky stretched wide above them. In the distance, the jagged peaks of the Blackridge Mountains loomed, their snow-capped summits glinting faintly in the sun.

"Men ahead!" came the sharp call of a scout.

Pesus raised his hand, narrowing his eyes as he spotted movement in a shallow dip ahead. A group of thirty men milled about, their armour catching the sunlight. They bore a banner—a silver eagle on a field of blue.

"Volneer's colours," Bones muttered as he rode up beside Pesus. "What are they doing here?"

Pesus frowned, his unease deepening. "Volneer has been our ally for years. But this far south?" He signalled for the column to halt. "Hold position."

Urging his horse forward, Pesus rode ahead, alone,

toward the group. He raised a hand in greeting. "Grand Marshal of Epiris" he called out. "State your business in these lands—"

His words were cut short as an arrow hissed through the air. Pesus ducked, the projectile glancing off his shoulder plate before embedding itself in the dirt behind him.

"Ambush!" Pesus roared, wheeling his horse around and galloping back to the column.

"Cavalry, forward!" he barked, his voice sharp and commanding.

Pax was already moving. "Charge!" he bellowed, raising his sword high as his cavalry surged forward.

The thunder of hooves shook the ground as the mounted soldiers closed the distance with brutal precision. The thirty men barely had time to react before the cavalry struck, their lances punching through shields and armour. The clash of steel rang out across the plain, and within minutes, the skirmish was over.

Bones dismounted, his boots sinking into the blood-soaked earth. Scanning the bodies, he found one man still alive, his breath ragged and his face pale with pain.

"This one's breathing" Bones growled, dragging the man upright and tossing him onto the ground.

Pesus approached, his face grim. "Why did you attack us?"

The man coughed, blood bubbling at the corners of his mouth. "Please... just end it..."

Bones planted a boot on the man's chest wound, pressing down hard enough to make him cry out. "Not until you talk," he said coldly. "Who gave the order to fire on the Grand Marshal?"

The soldier writhed, his voice trembling. "A captain... from Epiris... told King Volneer... your King Althern betrayed his father King Apius and his brother Rok… killed them both…"

Bones's face darkened. "That's a lie."

The man gasped, his voice fading. "Volneer… and Asos… they're joining forces… they'll crush Epiris before… your king turns on them too…"

Bones's grip on his sword tightened. Without hesitation, he swung, ending the soldier's life with a single, swift strike.

Pesus stood silently, the soldier's words hanging heavily in the air.

"This was a watch post," he said at last, his voice low. "If Volneer and Asos are joining forces, their armies could already be crossing Blackridge."

Bones looked toward the mountains, his jaw clenched. "Then they'll come down on Epiris like a hammer on an anvil."

Pesus exhaled slowly, the weight of the situation settling over him. "We need to move. Fast. If we're caught at the foot of the mountains, we'll be slaughtered."

The column pressed onward, their pace quickening. The jagged peaks of the Blackridge loomed closer with every step, their dark shadows stretching long across the plains.

Far to the west, the banners of Epiris still flew proudly above the city walls. But as Pesus rode in grim silence, his mind churned with questions. How many men awaited them? How much time did they have? And could Epiris stand against the combined might of two kings?

The march continued, the shadow of war growing heavier with every step.

About the Author

An avid reader of historical fiction, Alexander has always been captivated by eras ripe for interpretation and imagination. With a keen interest in world-building, Alexander enjoys crafting vivid landscapes and intricate settings inspired by real places visited. Every new location explored serves as a potential backdrop, breathing life into the pages of their work.

Character creation is a particular passion, as Alexander relishes shaping personalities that readers can connect with—flawed, layered, and undeniably human. The inspiration behind *Trinity of Thorns: Blood and Betrayal* stems from a deep fascination with the dynamics of power and authority, exploring how they can corrupt and create conflict between former allies. Beneath the intrigue and turmoil, the story carries a simple yet profound message: the importance of striving to be a good person amidst chaos.

When not writing, Alexander can be found roaming the moors with two loyal companions, Bella and Molly, or planning day trips to uncover new and inspiring locations. With over a decade of service working for the Crown, Alexander brings a nuanced perspective to tales of loyalty, betrayal, and the complexities of leadership.